CliffToppers
THE FIRE BAY
ADVENTURE

LONDON BOROUGH OF BARNET

D0281242

CLIFFTOPPERS

Have you read?

THE ARROWHEAD MOOR ADVENTURE

Look out for:

THE THORN ISLAND ADVENTURE

CLIFFTOPPERS
THE FIRE BAY
ADVENTURE

FLEUR HITCHCOCK

First published in the UK in 2019 by Nosy Crow Ltd
The Crow's Nest, 14 Baden Place
Crosby Row, London SE1 1YW, UK

Nosy Crow and associated logos are trademarks and/or registered
trademarks of Nosy Crow Ltd

Text copyright © Fleur Hitchcock, 2019
Cover illustration copyright © Tom Clohosy Cole, 2019

The right of Fleur Hitchcock to be identified as the author of this work has
been asserted by her in accordance with the Copyright, Designs
and Patents Act 1988.

All rights reserved

1 3 5 7 9 10 8 6 4 2

A CIP catalogue record for this book is available from the British Library.

This book is sold subject to the condition that it shall not, by way of
trade or otherwise, be lent, hired out or otherwise circulated in any
form of binding or cover other than that in which it is published. No
part of this publication may be reproduced, stored in a retrieval
system, or transmitted in any form or by any means (electronic, mechanical,
photocopying, recording or otherwise) without the prior written permission
of Nosy Crow Ltd.

Printed and bound in Great Britain by Clays Ltd, Elcograf S.p.A.
Typeset by Tiger Media

Papers used by Nosy Crow are made from wood grown in
sustainable forests.

ISBN: 978 1 78800 061 1

www.nosycrow.com

For Lewin and Rosa

CHAPTER 1

The four cousins had eaten the sandwiches laid out for them before Grandpa even had a chance to change his shoes.

"Delicious," announced Aiden, scraping chutney from his chin.

"Mmm," said Josh through the crumbs. He pointed at his sister's plate. "D'you want that?"

"Off," said Ava, waving him away and stuffing a last chunk of cheese in her mouth.

Chloe said nothing. She was just enjoying sitting at the table with her cousins, her grandparents and Bella the dog, and feeling the expanse of the holiday stretching in front of her. She was an only child, and this was the nearest she ever got to having brothers and sisters. Josh was younger than her, only eight. She was nine, Aiden was eleven and Ava, Josh's older sister, was twelve. But age didn't matter here at Clifftopper Farm. Anyone could do anything, and everyone listened to everyone else.

They'd all just arrived from different parts of the country, and in a minute they would go down and investigate the bonfire that was being built for the annual Drake's Bay Fire Festival tomorrow. Chloe was excited because she'd never been allowed to go before.

"All full?" said Grandpa. "Ready, Primrose?"

"Ready," said Grandma Primrose, taking a coat from a peg and jamming a woolly hat on her grey curls. "Bella, lead the way."

As they followed Bella down to Drake's Bay village, the sea and the sky were both dull grey, with a thin sliver of greeny orange dividing them. Lights were coming on in the village below, strings of coloured bulbs laced between the houses, and a pool of yellow from the harbour-master's office warmed the quayside. Chloe shivered and thrust her hands into the pockets. It was chilly up here on the hill.

"Beautiful," said Ava under her breath, and in her head Chloe agreed.

Being here always made Chloe feel good. It was all that emptiness, all that nature with no cars racing around. It was so calm. There were boats idling out at sea, their masts clanking. Seagulls slowly floated back into land, and people were stomping about on the beach, but it was all distant. Mellow.

"Bliss," she replied eventually.

"Almost makes up for my broken Nintendo," said Josh beside her.

"I'm not gonna lie, Josh — it was your fault," said Ava.

"Wasn't," he snapped.

"Was," she said. "You were the one that sat on it."

"You could have warned me," he said. "It was on the seat next to you."

Ava sighed.

Josh sighed.

Chloe looked back at the view. It *was* still very peaceful here. Even with Josh around.

They wandered through the village, and as they grew closer to the beach Chloe gradually noticed the stack of wood right in the middle. From the top of the hill it had blended in with the pebbles, but now they were nearly there she could see what it really was. There was driftwood of course, but also in the heap were broken chairs, benches, cupboards, pallets, and bits of boat, all tangled together. Chloe stared, wondering just how massive the flames would be and if it was really a good idea to set fire to so much so close to the village, and if it was really necessary to set fire to all the driftwood because she knew her mum would have liked to have it and turn it into a mirror or something.

"Race you to the arch, Aiden," said Ava as they stepped on to the beach, and she pelted off over the pebbles towards the stone arch at the end of the beach, Aiden and Bella in hot pursuit.

Josh ran two paces after his sister, and then, deciding that she'd win anyway, stopped and turned back to walk with Chloe, who was slowly heading towards the bonfire in the middle of the beach. They passed a mum and her daughter, sitting on a rock, arguing.

"But Mum, it's fifteen pounds. Just fifteen pounds. Those things cost like, loads, and I really, really want it. It's made by Xarca – they're like, really, really good."

Josh paused. *Xarca?*

"What?" asked Chloe.

"They're talking about Xarca – the best ever makers of electronics," he whispered. "Why would they be talking about them here? In Drake's Bay?"

"But what is it exactly?" said the mum. "And why would you need such a thing?"

Josh shuffled closer.

"It's a VR headset. Virtual reality, Mum." The girl sounded really excited. "It's not one of those stupid ones where you put the phone inside, it's a proper one where you're in the world itself and you can, like –" she whirled her arms around – "shoot things all around you! Pleeeeeease? And I bet you'd use it. It'd give us hours and hours of fun. And I promise I won't not go for walks and stuff, it's just sooooooo. Oh!"

Her mother laughed. "Goodness – I suppose so, and what about your friends? Will you let them use it?"

Unable to keep quiet any longer, Josh stepped over to them.

"'S'cuse me, but are there VR headsets in Drake's Bay? Where?"

The girl frowned at Josh and looked up at her mum.

"Hello," said the mum. "Apparently, there's a man in the market, or he was there today, who sells virtual-reality headsets. And he's going to be there tomorrow morning too." She tilted her head towards her daughter. "And Jasmine wants to buy one."

"Did you say fifteen pounds?" said Josh. "Like, one-five?"

The girl nodded.

"Whooooo," Josh let out a long sigh. "Magic." Leaving Chloe, he ran to look for Grandma.

"Grandma, could you please, please, please give me fifteen pounds so that I can buy a virtual-reality headset? It's this kind of magic thing that you put on your head that lets you play computer—"

"No, Josh, certainly not," she said, without even pausing to think about it. "Evening, Jake," she called over Josh's head. "How's it going?"

"But, Grandma!"

"Oh, hello, Primrose," Jake replied. Jake was a local fisherman, who right now was directing a man with a wheelbarrow of trellis with one hand and scooping his nets into a heap with the other. "Here – this side." The man emptied his wheelbarrow on the heap.

"So much … stuff!" said Aiden, strolling back from the end of the beach. "Was it this big last year?"

"It's definitely bigger!" called Ava. "And more coming all the time."

"It's going to be huge," said Chloe.

"When do the tar barrels come in?" asked Josh, trying really hard to feel happy about the bonfire, and not furious with Grandma, although, to be fair, he knew she would never give him fifteen pounds. Certainly not for technology. She might give him fifteen pounds for an encylopedia, or a football.

Jake laughed. "Keen to carry one then,

pipsqueak?" He ruffled Josh's hair.

"Can I?" asked Josh, ignoring the hair ruffle and putting on his sweetest most charming face.

"You have a snowball's chance in hell, young man," said Grandma, laying a restraining hand on Josh's shoulder. "This is the first year that Chloe's mum has said she can come to the celebrations – I'm not letting you, as an eight-year-old, carry a flaming tar barrel on your head.

"Oh Grandma! Please? If I can't buy a VR headset, at least let me—"

"Definitely not."

"Grandpa?" Josh fluttered his eyelashes at his grandfather.

"I think it's a no, Josh," he replied. "Your mother would never forgive us. Ava on the other hand..."

"Me?" said Ava. "I'd love to!"

Josh shot her a look that he hoped she would understand as a deadly threat. No way was he going to let his sister get away with barrel carrying if he couldn't. "That is totally unfair," he said.

"It isn't at all unfair," said Grandma. "Now, Josh, I just need to explain the difference between eight years old and twelve years old." Grandma swept him round to the other side of the bonfire and shook her finger at him rather more seriously than he had expected.

CHAPTER 2

Ava watched her brother trying hard to persuade Grandma and Grandpa that he was, actually, older than eight. *Had Grandpa meant it? Was she actually old enough to be allowed to carry a barrel?*

"So how does the tar barrel thing work?" Chloe asked Jake.

"Starts at the church," Jake replied.

"Then," butted in a woman, who Ava knew was Pearl, the kayak-hire lady, "the runners lift the barrels on to their heads…"

"And we set fire to them," said Jake.

"Seriously?" asked Chloe. "Isn't that dangerous? Doesn't their hair catch light?"

"Special woven fireproof headgear." Jake laughed. "We've learned our lesson with that one."

"They come down the high street," said Pearl.

"On to the beach," continued Jake.

"And roll them up to the bonfire," finished Pearl.

"Sounds brilliant," said Chloe. "I'm so glad Mum's letting me go this year."

"And then the fireworks go off," said Aiden.

"Oh yeah, the fireworks," Ava said, remembering last year's amazing display. "They're double good because they go off over the sea. Reflections. The whole thing's pretty awesome. Especially the barrel bit." Ava said it extra loudly, just to make sure that everyone knew how much she wanted to carry one.

"Glad you think so," said Pearl, lugging a wooden sawhorse up to the pile.

"But why?" asked Chloe. "I get the bonfire and the fireworks, that's like everywhere, but the barrels?"

"Well, they're not filled with brandy any more,"

said Pearl, as if that explained everything.

"And that's why that end of the beach is called Fire Bay, while the rest of all of this –" Jake waved his hands at the sea – "is Drake's Bay. See?"

"Uh?" said Chloe.

"It's to keep the ghosts away," said Ava. "They used to burn blue – because they were full of brandy, like Christmas cakes."

"It's all about the ghosts," said Grandma, stomping towards them over the shingle with a slightly miserable Josh in tow. "Blue ghosts."

"I didn't know it was for the ghosts," said Josh, his voice very slightly wobbly. "If they don't burn the barrels do the ghosts appear?"

"What?" Chloe looked very confused.

Pearl laughed, and lowered herself on to a log. "So, hundreds of years ago, there was this sound – a booming sound. It echoed through the village night after night. People couldn't sleep. It made the children cry and the old people pray. Some people said it was a whale. Others said it was waves crashing in an underwater cave, a log caught in the undertow. But most people thought it was because of the ghostly shipwreck out here in Fire Bay." She pointed across to some small rocks that stuck out from the sea at the end of the beach. "Some years earlier, one awful stormy night, a smuggler's lugger was wrecked on the reef and a few small barrels of brandy floated in through the storm. They were alight. Burning with a blue flame. But when the men went to search the wreck of the boat the next day, expecting to find the rest of the shipment, there was no one there. No sign of any brandy neither." Pearl paused and looked around.

Josh let out a little whimper. "I didn't know that," he said, very quietly.

Pearl continued. "The ship was empty. The villagers decided that it must have been attacked at sea, the brandy mostly stolen, the crew gone overboard. That the lit barrels were a lesson to any smugglers."

There was silence.

Although she'd heard it a hundred times, Ava felt a shiver run down her spine and Josh slipped his hand into hers.

"Or," said Aiden, loudly into the silence, "the crew crept on to the land with some of the brandy, while the people were distracted by the flaming barrels, and then they tiptoed home in the darkness."

"You mean the smugglers double-crossed the villagers?" asked Chloe.

"Good idea, Aiden," said Grandpa. "They were all crooks – why not?"

"The villagers kept a watch all night and all day, they say," said Pearl. "No one saw hide nor hair of the smugglers. No one was ever seen. The missing men, the missing brandy and the booming remain a mystery to this day."

"So there's no other way off the beach," said Chloe.

"Unless…" said Pearl. "Unless, the rumours of a smugglers' tunnel are true."

Josh immediately started back across the beach towards the huge cliffs, now glowing slightly pink in the last of the light. "Why didn't you ever tell us about the smugglers' tunnel?" he shouted.

"Didn't we?" said Grandpa.

"Sure we did," said Grandma.

"Did you ever look for it, Pearl?" asked Ava, gazing up at the rocky wall, scouring every lump and bump for signs of a cave entrance. There were caves on the other side of the harbour – why not here? Perhaps Pearl and Jake hadn't been very good at looking.

"Course. Spent our childhoods looking for it, didn't we, Jake? All summer long, searching for that thing."

"Never found anything," said Jake, threading a broom handle into the pile.

"Nor I," said Grandma. "All the years we've lived here, not a hint of a tunnel."

"Or a ghostly boom!" added Grandpa.

Pearl glanced over at the cliff. "Gotta be there somewhere though."

"Oh?" said Ava.

"Stands to reason, don't it?" said Jake.

"No smoke without fire," replied Pearl, staring wistfully along the beach. "I longed to find it when I was your age."

"So you really think it exists?" asked Aiden, taking his glasses off and cleaning them on his sweatshirt. "Can you see anything over there, Ava? I wish I could see better in the dark."

"Well I'm going home to put the dinner on," said Grandpa. "Coming, Primrose?"

Grandma smiled and took Grandpa's hand.

"Happy hunting – see you at home in an hour or so?"

But Ava had followed Josh and was running towards the rock face, even though all that could now be seen of the cliffs was a gentle rose glow.

In the end, darkness won, and they gave up looking. But not before Josh had been convinced that he'd found the entrance, and Bella had disappeared halfway up the cliff and reappeared some time later chasing a gull.

"So she definitely said VR," said Josh, teetering on the edge of the sea wall. "But Grandma's not going to help me get one. I mean, wasted opportunity or what?"

"They're probably pretend ones," said Ava. "You know, like those little mobile phones kids have."

"Are you sure the girl said Xarca?" said Aiden. "They don't make kids' stuff – they're a really good brand."

Josh let out a long sigh. "Fifteen pounds is nothing. People pay, like, loads for them. Hundreds."

They walked on a little further. "Have you got fifteen pounds, sis?" he asked.

"No," said Ava.

"Nor have I," said Chloe quickly.

"Me neither," said Aiden.

"Poo," said Josh. "And they're not going to let me carry a barrel."

"Are you surprised?" asked Chloe.

"No," said Josh, mournfully, pointing at Ava. "But they'll let *her* carry one."

"We don't know that," said Ava. "Grandma hasn't said I can. Nor's Pearl."

"They will though, won't they?" said Josh, and then he let out the longest, most unhappy sigh.

He was so dismal that he didn't seem to notice the first fire engine stopping at the top of the hill.

A couple of minutes later, another joined it.

Ava had to poke him to get him to run at all.

CHAPTER 3

Aiden followed Ava and they half ran, half walked up through the village, chasing the blue lights that bounced from hedges and walls ahead of them. He could smell smoke and hear the distant crackle of fire.

"Look!" yelled Chloe, pointing up the hill towards the post office.

She didn't need to point. Ominous orange flames were licking around the sides of the thatched roof that hung low over the post-office windows and small sparks of burned straw shot high into the midnight sky. A ladder from the first fire engine was already resting against an upper-floor window and a woman was handing a child out of the window to a waiting fireman. Water poured over everything from a giant hose, and clouds of steam and smoke rose from the building. But it wasn't just the post office that was on fire. The storage yard next door was also on fire. And next to that was the village petrol station and twenty thousand gallons of petrol and a lorry load of gas canisters.

"Mind out!" shouted Chloe as a third fire engine howled its way into the village, screeching to a halt ahead of them.

Firefighters leaped from the truck and ran straight into the yard to tackle the growing flames. "Keep back!" they yelled as they ran.

"Let's get out of here," said Ava, grabbing Bella's collar and heading down the street. "That petrol station's not safe."

The four cousins darted back through the narrow gap between the fire engines, raced under the drifting sparks and stopped on the far side of the post office. Below them the village looked normal. Dark, with squares of yellow light. But up the hill everything was lit by the awful orange glow of the burning thatch and the high street was blocked by fire engines and firefighters and fire.

"We could walk home over the fields," said Chloe as the rain of sparks doubled. "It might be safer."

They wandered a little further back down into Drake's Bay and the sounds changed from the roar of the fire to the ordinary clattering of masts and slopping of the tide.

Crash…

"What's that?" shouted Ava.

The sound came again. Glass shattering followed by thumping, and was that shouting? Bella sniffed the air and then let out a growl.

"Think it came from down here," yelled Josh, disappearing down a flight of steps that led to the harbour. Ava followed, Chloe too, and then Bella.

"Hang on!" In the dark Aiden struggled to keep up and a second later he tripped into a stack of lobster pots that had been left on the side of the steps.

"Ow!" He sat down and rubbed his ankle, peering into the gloom ahead. He could just about make out the darker silhouettes of the others but he always struggled in the dark because of his spectacles. A moment later Bella raced back towards him, but she didn't stop. She shot down another alleyway off to the side.

"Bella – come here!" He listened for her claws on the cobbles but now all he could hear was the sea.

Wobbling to his feet, he limped a little closer to the harbourside. The orange of the burning post office reflected in the water and for a moment he thought how lovely it looked.

Crash!

It was that breaking glass again. And this time it was much closer.

"Help!" It was a feeble cry, but it came from his left. Bella appeared from the same direction, barked at him, and ran back into complete darkness.

Aiden swung around. He wished he could see better at night. Bella could obviously see exactly what was going on, but he peered, trying to make sense of the dark shapes in front of him. Two very black things flanked the alleyway. They must be the tall fish warehouses, but between them was a less black thing. A gap that led into a space that he'd never noticed before. A courtyard. It didn't seem to have any electric lighting, but the cobbles shone from the glow of a small window. A small orange window of flames.

Fire? Again?

Aiden ran towards it. The crashing noise must have been the panes of glass exploding outwards because something crunched under his feet. He could feel the heat.

"Help!" The call was louder.

"Where are you?" he shouted into the dark.

Bella growled and barked and ran in circles.

"Up here!"

He couldn't see it at first, but there, above and to the side, was another window. Aiden was unsure if it was open or closed, and he couldn't work out if the smudge he could see was a face or arms or what, but he knew it was too high to jump from, the cobbles too hard to fall on. He looked back at the ground floor. There was a door by the flaming window. The wood surround was already starting to burn. And inside, flames were licking around what he took to be the staircase. There was no way anyone was going to get out downstairs.

"Hang on!" he shouted, frantically feeling his

way around the bottoms of the walls in case there was a ladder or anything that would help. All he found were some giant hooks at shoulder height that must have been used to dry nets sometime in ancient history. Nothing else. Nothing helpful. Briefly he thought of running for the fire engine. But there was no way he'd get up there and make himself understood, nor was there any way the fire engine would be able to get down here.

"We're going to have to jump!" came the voice, and then a child crying.

"NO – don't. Wait!" Aiden had a thought. "Wait a second!"

CHAPTER 4

Turning and running from the alley, he swung to his right. *Yes!* Here were the lobster pots he'd fallen over, loads of them, and nets. He grabbed three, dropped one because they were so heavy, then dragged them down the steps and along the alley and dumped them under the window, Bella at his side.

"I'm getting some stuff for you to land on!" he shouted, running back for more. "But don't jump yet."

"What?" shouted another voice. "What have you got?"

"Lobster pots, wicker ones!" he shouted back.

"Be quick!" yelled the voice.

"I will. Ava! Josh! Chloe!" Aiden called into the dark while running back to the pile of lobster pots. Bella ran to the top of the steps and began to bark into the dark. "Bella, that's just not helpful," he muttered, loading himself with three more wicker cages and a net. He was scuttling back down the alley with them when Ava appeared out of the dark. "Quick! Lobster pots, nets on the steps, drag them down – people…" He pointed breathlessly at the dark window above the flames.

Ava didn't even speak, but vanished, and a moment later, just as Aiden was trying to arrange the pots in the dark, she reappeared with Josh and Chloe and the remainder of the stuff.

"Will this work?" asked Ava, hurriedly stacking the cages on top of each other so that they covered the bottom of the courtyard. Sparks shot out of the broken window, but luckily the lobster pots were too wet to catch fire. They'd made a floor of the lobster pots. It wasn't soft, but it was a lot softer than cobbles. Aiden just hoped it would stop anyone breaking anything.

"I think they should jump," said Chloe. "Look!"

Aiden looked up. Flames had now appeared in another upstairs window, and a second later the glass blew out.

"How many of you are there?" shouted Ava.

"Four. And a cat!" shouted the voice.

"The baskets'll crush," muttered Aiden. "We need something more to break their fall." And then he had another thought. He remembered the hooks he'd found earlier. They were all the way around the courtyard. If they could just catch the side of one of the big nets on the hooks, they could make a kind of trampoline.

"What are you doing?" said Ava, her face now quite clear in the firelight.

"We gotta jump!" shouted the first voice.

"Wait!" yelled Aiden. "Hooks," he said. "The hooks in the walls!"

Catching on, Josh and Ava scrambled over the nets and managed to attach two sides of a net, while Aiden hooked the third side under the window. The fourth flopped over the lobster pots beneath it.

"We're jumping!" shouted the voice.

Aiden ran for the loose side of the net.

"Aaaaah!" came a shout and someone or something bounced on to the net. Aiden was jerked forward, his fingers stinging from clinging so tight, but he pulled back on the net again, joined by Ava, Josh and Chloe and then by whoever it was that had jumped. Somebody in their pyjamas.

"Jump, Tom!" yelled the small person standing next to him, and there was another jolt as someone fell into the net. That person scrambled to the side and something small and black and squealing fell from the window.

"Mr Tibbs!" shouted one of the rescued children, and the black thing scratched its way to the side of the net and shot past Aiden's legs, closely followed by Bella.

"Mum!" shouted one of the children.

This time, they were all yanked forward and Aiden cracked heads with Ava, but the woman scrambled to the side of the net, got to her feet and grabbed at the net to steady it.

"David!" she shouted, and the last person leaped.

The net tore and for a moment Aiden wondered

if he'd lost one of his fingers, but the man bounced to his feet, running away from the building, grabbing for his children.

"Run, run," he shouted, pushing Aiden in front of him. "Run!"

And Aiden ran, shoving Josh through the gap that led to the steps.

As he turned the corner, the front of the building blew out.

CHAPTER 5

"Boy," said the dad.

"Not joking," said the mum, hugging her daughter. "We're so grateful," she said, giving Aiden a hug. "Just think. You are an absolute hero!"

Aiden flushed deep red. "What about the cat?" he asked, changing the subject.

"Oh no! Mr Tibbs – he did jump, didn't he?" asked the mum.

"Yes." Chloe looked down at Bella. The last time anyone had seen Mr Tibbs was when Bella shot out of the alley, chasing him. She didn't look a bit guilty and was much more interested in sniffing at the firemen's legs. "But I'm afraid I didn't see where he went next."

"Stand back please!" shouted one of the firefighters as hot masonry crumbled into the street.

"Let's get out of the way," said Ava, clambering up the steps past the remains of the lobster pots.

The little boy began to cry. "Mr Tibbs, where's Mr Tibbs?"

"I'm sure he'll be fine," said the dad, following Ava. "The main thing is that we're fine, and we know Mr Tibbs jumped clear. I bet someone'll find him."

"Do you know what started the fire?" Chloe asked, dragging Bella away from whatever was on the fireman's boot that she found so interesting.

"It wasn't anything that I can think of," said the mum.

"Pretty sure we put the kettle on once or twice but we made tea, so it must have switched off or we'd have noticed. Were you playing on your computer game thingy, Tom?"

"Not when the fire happened. It was downstairs,"

said the boy. "I'm tired, Mum – where are we gonna sleep?"

"So'm I," whined the girl.

A policeman arrived, sweeping the family ahead of him towards the hotel at the bottom of the hill.

"Let's get out of here," said Aiden, rounding the corner and heading up the hill towards the glowing embers of the post-office roof.

"Two fires in one evening," said Chloe. "Don't you think that's kind of weird?"

"Very," said Aiden.

"I wonder…" said Chloe. "I wonder if we could talk to the people in the post office?"

"Well, they won't be there any more, will they?" said Ava, pointing at the ruins.

"Stinks," said Josh.

And it did. Burned wet straw – like fish, Chloe thought. Smoked fish. And Ava was right. There were only police and firefighters around. The actual post-office residents had disappeared.

"There you are!" It was Grandpa, followed shortly after by Grandma Primrose, who stared at the remains of the post office in horror.

"Oh my word!" she said. "We heard the fire

engines – no idea it would be as bad as this."

"You should see the house down the road!" said Josh. "We saved a whole family."

"Including their cat," said Chloe.

"Well, Aiden did," said Ava. "It was Aiden who rescued them, really – we just helped a bit."

In the dark, Chloe couldn't see the colour of Aiden's face, but she was pretty sure it was bright red.

The smell of the fire followed them all the way back to Clifftoppers, and all the way back they talked of Mr Tibbs but never spotted him. Ava charged up the stairs to have the first shower and it took ages to get Josh out of his, so Chloe was absolutely ravenous by the time they'd all changed into pyjamas and Grandpa said it was time to eat.

"Sit up!" announced Grandpa, taking a plum crumble out of the oven.

Grandma looked slightly anxious.

"What is it, dear?" asked Grandpa, rustling in the freezer in search of ice cream.

"I think," said Grandma. "I think we had better

be quiet about this evening. Chloe's mum might have a fit if she heard what you children did."

"We just helped some people escape," said Josh.

"We witnessed the fire," said Ava.

"Saved a cat?" suggested Aiden.

Chloe imagined her mother's reaction to any of that. "Perhaps we should say nothing?"

"Good idea," said Grandma, smiling. "Now, who wants crumble?"

"There is an upside," said Ava to Chloe, as they lay in bed later that night.

"Oh?" said Chloe, thinking of the devastated post office, the homeless family, the cat.

"Josh seems to have forgotten all about the stupid headset thingy."

"He has, hasn't he?" Chloe thought back through the evening. Working through everything that had happened, everything she'd learned. "Thing is," she said. "I think they're definitely connected."

"What?" said Ava. "The barrels and the fire?"

"I hadn't thought of that," said Chloe. "No – the two fires this evening. The post office and the one with the family."

Ava lay silent for a while. "I suppose it's quite a coincidence."

"There's that, and…"

"What?"

"The mum asked the boy if he'd been playing his computer game."

Chloe heard Ava turn over and knew that she was now facing her across the bedroom. "Yes, and?"

"Well, maybe she meant VR."

Again, there was a long silence. "Ye-es, maybe."

"And at the fire in the flat above the post office, we saw that woman passing a kid out of the window. So there's a chance that kid had a VR headset too."

"Mm-hmm…"

"You don't think I'm right?"

"I dunno," said Ava. "I really don't."

"I just feel that there's something…"

There was a long pause.

"Let's talk about it in the morning."

CHAPTER 6

Josh was out of bed before the others. He was waiting at the breakfast table when Chloe came down, he had his shoes on before Grandpa Edward had delivered the first hash brown, and he had eaten every scrap of his breakfast before Ava had even started hers. Aiden had convinced him that he needed to get a good look at one of the headsets before he even thought about buying one, but that didn't stop him imagining what it would be like to wear one.

He'd be inside a world; it would be all around his

head. He wouldn't just move his hand; he'd move his whole arm. His whole body. He'd always wanted one. Well, he'd wanted one for nearly a month. And since he'd sat on his Nintendo yesterday on the train, he'd say he actually needed one.

"Can we go down to the harbour now?" he asked, his tongue practically hanging out.

"Wait, Josh," said his sister. "Let me at least have some toast."

"And I'd be very grateful if you could get that wood I collected yesterday down to the bonfire today," said Grandpa Edward, pausing mid-egg flip. "I think if you do it together you can drag it all down in one go and give it to Jake." He stopped and looked up. "You are all still happy about the bonfire, aren't you?"

"I'd be happier if I could carry a barrel," mumbled Josh.

"Yeah, totally," said Ava. "Looking forward to it. Especially the barrel bit."

"It's so much fun carrying a barrel," said Grandma. "Did it two or three times, didn't I, Edward?"

"A veritable champion," smiled Grandpa

Edward, kissing the top of Grandma's head.

With some satisfaction, Josh noticed that neither of them actually said anything about Ava carrying a barrel.

Grandma wiped a blob of marmalade from her chin. "Anyway, Grandpa's made you a small picnic. Egg sandwiches for you, Chloe, ham for the rest of you," she said, handing Aiden a bag.

Grandpa reached into his back pocket for his wallet and took out a twenty-pound note. "Here's some money for pasties. You might need them, the picnic's only emergency rations. The café's open all day."

Josh waited in a state close to agony for everyone to decide what they were going to wear, for Grandpa to give them all gloves for dragging the wood, for Ava to change her coat twice and end up wearing the same one she'd started with.

"Ava!" he said.

"Yes, Josh? What?"

Eventually they left the farmyard, ropes fastened around a pallet that Grandpa was donating to the bonfire and, balanced on top, a broken chair, a one-legged table, a woodwormed milking stool, three rotting apple crates, half a cot and about a million old baskets. Josh walked in front, warning cars that they were coming. Ava and Aiden did the first shift of dragging, sometimes with the ropes over their shoulders, sometimes just tugging at it. Chloe walked at the back, picking up the things that fell off. Which was plenty.

Then they all swapped, and Josh tried to speed things up, except Chloe got cross with him for going too fast and they got uneven and half the things fell off and Bella ran away with the end of the cot, and then Ava got cross and the sun came out and they all got hot, but eventually, they made it to the harbour.

"No!" said Ava as Josh dropped the rope.

"What?" said Josh, looking around at the others.

"No – you can't go sneaking off and leave us to get this to the beach," said his sister with something that Josh felt was very nearly smugness.

"I just—"

"Ava's right," said Aiden. "If you want to see the man with the VR headsets then he'll still be there in ten minutes. Come on, help us."

"Come on, Josh," said Chloe.

Rather than call his sister names, a long string of names that she would probably report back to Grandma, or, even worse, Mum, he let out a long breath and kicked the pallet hard. Kicking the pallet tipped it slightly, setting in motion a slow avalanche of crates and baskets. This was why they finally arrived at the bonfire site twenty minutes later than they had originally intended, and why Josh only reached the market as Jasmine, the girl he'd seen arguing with her mum on the beach the day before, was leaving with a box clutched to her chest and an enormous grin.

"Thank you, Mum," she said. "Race you back to the chalet." She saw Josh and frowned, clutching her VR set close to her chest. Then, for no reason at all, she stuck her tongue out at him.

Josh ran past her to find that the man with the headsets was packing up.

"Sold out," he said.

"What?" said Josh. "But it's only half past nine! How could you?"

"Came with twenty-five. Sold twenty-five. Sold out, mate. Told you." The man didn't even look up.

Josh stood there, his mouth open, trying to understand what the man had just said as he watched him taking his stand down and cramming the table and gazebo into the back of a van.

"But you've got some in there – I can see them!" said Josh.

"Nah, mate – those are just boxes. Boxes, see?" He held one up in front of Josh's face long enough for him to see the Xarca logo, but not long enough for him to actually get his hands on it.

"But are you coming back?" said Josh, following the man back and forth to the van.

"No, mate, no. Sold out."

"You mean, *sold out*, sold out – like you've totally absolutely run out?"

"Yes. Now – get out of the way like a good boy. I need to get out of here."

"How much are they?"

"Next time, thirty quid each."

"But!" Josh pointed at a battered sign that read £15.

"Yes, but it's the trader's prerogative to set the price, and demand and supply sets the price, and there's a bigger demand than supply, so next time – thirty quid."

"That's…" Josh couldn't think of the word, but he thought it began with an "e" – "ex … something."

The man threw the sign in the back of the van. But Josh wouldn't let it go.

"So, if there's a next time, will there be more? Like, on Wednesday or something?"

The man stopped and leaned against the back of the van, looking at Josh as if seeing him properly for the first time. "I am, as it happens, waiting for a shipment. In which case—"

"When will that be?" asked Josh, not trusting himself to look the man in the eye and instead focusing on a frayed length of yellow nylon string tied to the back-door handle of the van.

"I don't know," the man said, speaking really slowly as if Josh was only two years old. Josh noticed the man's greasy hair hung down the same length all the way round his head. He looked like a mushroom.

"But soon," suggested Josh.

"Maybe yes, maybe no. But anyway, I'm going to be selling those ones over in Porthmerron. Now…"

the man said, opening the driver's door and sitting down, "I want to get home to my lovely lady wife. And you, son, are in my way."

Josh stood away, trying to hide his disappointment. He put a studied scowl on his face and sniffed back an unwanted tear. The man ground the gears and reversed over the cobbles. In a fit of fury Josh pulled his red notebook from his pocket and wrote down the number plate and a description of the man. *Hairy, mushroom-head hair, rude, grey eyes, yellow teeth.* And as an afterthought he scribbled: *Extortion.* He jammed the notebook back in his pocket and stomped off to pop seaweed and throw pebbles in the sea.

CHAPTER 7

Once Josh had run off to the market, the whole time she was helping unload the burnables from the pallet and slot them into the bonfire, Ava was thinking of what Chloe had said. Was it more than coincidence?

"Here's the hero of the hour!" said Jake, ambling along the beach, dragging a branch. He stopped and slapped Aiden on the back.

Ava noticed that Aiden went bright red.

"Not just me," he said, poking Ava, "She helped, and the others."

"Well, from what I heard, it was your quick thinking that saved them," said Jake.

"It was," agreed Ava.

"Have you seen it in the daylight?" asked Pearl, joining them. "Just a shell of a place," she said. "Nothing but walls and a roof this morning. Shocking."

"Just as well I left my lobster pots there cluttering up the alley," said Jake.

"It was," said Aiden, going an even deeper red.

"I'm proud of you, kids," said Pearl. "Just marvellous, what you did."

"Brilliant stuff," said Jake, wandering off to the harbour.

Ava watched him go, and over his head saw a white van wiggle slowly up the high street through the haze of smoke still hanging around the post office.

"Anyway!" said Aiden, his ears tomato red, his glasses foggy. "Must go and ... look for that cat." He began to walk away over the beach. Chloe trotted after him.

"Cat?" Pearl asked as Ava moved to follow them.

"Yup. We need to find a cat – Mr Tibbs. A black

cat that went missing last night during the fire. Have you seen it?" asked Ava, pretending to search the cliffs.

"No – but actually, Ava, love, I did mean to ask, did you want to carry a barrel in the festival? Got a few extras this year, unclaimed. You're tall enough, and with your hair in braids you'd be fine."

"Me?" said Ava imagining what it would be like to run through the town with a flaming barrel on her head. "Oh yes!" she said, "Although – it depends on Grandma."

"She carried them herself a few years ago, and your grandad," Pearl said thoughtfully. "I'll ask her."

Ava raced across the beach to catch up with the others. "Guess what? Pearl asked if I wanted to carry a barrel tomorrow." She felt the smile practically crack her face.

"Yay," said Aiden.

"Brilliant!" said Chloe. "Though I'm glad it's not me."

"Josh won't be happy," said Aiden.

"Where *is* Josh?" Ava said. "Not still hanging

around hoping to get a VR headset?"

"I do hope not," said Chloe.

"What do you mean?" asked Aiden.

"Chloe thinks they're all connected."

"The fires?"

"Yes," said Chloe, "the fires, but also the VR sets. It's just, we know that they're being sold very cheaply here – like, suspiciously cheaply – and suddenly there are a load of fires."

Aiden nodded as if he was slowly understanding what they'd said.

"So hopefully Josh hasn't magically found fifteen pounds to buy one too," said Ava.

"Exactly," said Chloe.

"Are you serious?" asked Aiden.

"Totally," said Chloe.

"Well, let's see if we can find the people from the post office," said Aiden. "If they bought one, then it's a start. If they didn't – then…" He shrugged.

"We could pretend that we're looking for the cat," said Chloe as they stomped up the hill from the beach towards the post office.

"We could ask the police if they've seen Mr

Tibbs, and maybe find out where the people from the post office are," said Ava.

Aiden looked at her as if she was mad. "Why not?" she said.

"What – like the people from the post office ran from the fire and grabbed the cat at the same time?"

"You got a better idea?" asked Ava.

They set off for the village, pretending to search for Mr Tibbs. Chloe made it more realistic by shouting "Mr Tibbs" at every alley and every shed door until Ava thought that she was overdoing it. They slowed as they reached the post office. Quite a crowd had formed, and there were people in yellow high-vis jackets and safety helmets pulling the burned thatch from the roof.

A white van was trying to get through the mass of people blocking the road.

"Keep back, keep back please," said a man in a helmet.

"Does anyone know where the people from the post office are?" asked Chloe. "It's just, they might have found a missing cat."

"They'll be down the road at the pub, love, or

they might be at the hotel. Or talking to the police by the warehouse fire."

Which is when the family they'd rescued appeared.

"We were so lucky that you came along. Just so lucky," said the dad. "Have you seen the place?"

"No — Jake and Pearl were just telling—" began Ava.

"You're such a hero!" said the mum, lunging towards Aiden, but he was quick to step back so there was an awkward gap.

Ava tried to fill it. "Have you found Mr Tibbs?" she asked.

The boy let out a wail. "He's lost forever."

"I'm sure he isn't," said the mum. "Let's go and get some ice cream, Tom."

"But it's cold," Tom said, being led away towards the café.

"Excuse me," said Chloe. "Did you by any chance buy a VR set from a man at the market?"

"We did, as it happens," said the mum.

"Told you!" hissed Chloe.

"But if you're wondering if that started the fire, we also had dinner by candlelight — so we might not have blown it out properly," said the dad.

"Oh!" said Ava.

"Oh indeed," said Aiden.

CHAPTER 8

"But the two fires are just a coincidence unless the people in the flat above the post office also bought a VR headset," said Aiden, trying to be fair. "And there's the candle."

The end of the courtyard was sealed off with blue police tape but people were moving around inside the burned-out building.

"I could go in and talk to a police officer now," said Chloe.

"I don't think you should," said Aiden. "It's a guess, AND you shouldn't contaminate the scene."

Ava laughed. "We were running all over it last night – with Bella!"

"OK. But I still don't think we should tell the police – yet. I mean – you are just guessing."

Ava sighed. "I get your point," she said, "but the chances of two fires in one night – here? In the middle of, like, nowhere?"

Aiden felt himself turn red for the third time that morning. He was still completely sure, though, that so far it looked like two accidents, no matter how weird and coincidental they were. Not two crimes. "Please?" he said in the end, wishing that the girls would just stop attracting attention. He didn't think he could take much more of it. He'd blush himself out of existence.

"Look, there's Josh," he said, changing the subject. "Let's see whether he got to meet the headset man."

In the distance Josh and Grandma crossed the high street towards the harbour. Josh looked furious and Grandma was obviously trying to calm him down.

A moment later Grandma went back the other way. This time without Josh.

The cousins wandered on down the alleyway towards the quayside.

"Well, I'm still sure that there's a connection, and I still think it's a good thing that Josh hasn't got any money," said Chloe. "I mean, imagine if the farmhouse went up in flames."

"Where's he gone?"

They stopped, overlooking the harbour.

A lone stall stood on the quayside. A blonde woman was struggling to put up a large sign that said *Xarca phones £20*. Behind her was a white van filled with small shiny boxes. In front of her was Josh, staring at the phones. He was deep in thought, examining the boxes. Beside him, Bella was scratching herself on the table, unaware of the effect she was having above her head where the piles of phones trembled.

"Twenty quid, genuine article – slightly soiled stock, one day only," the woman said. "Hey, what are you doing?"

"Oh, sorry," said Josh, pulling Bella away, who immediately went back to the table leg and continued to scratch her ear on the sticky-out bit. "Twenty quid?" said Josh. "For real?"

Aiden stopped. Xarca? Xarca again?

He wandered over and stood behind Josh, listening and watching the woman. "Here you are, sonny, absolute bargain. Totally brilliant phones. No signal down here of course, so there's no way of knowing how well they work, but take them up the hill and you'll be able to talk to your friends on the other side of the world clear as a bell. Twenty quid – cheap at twice the price!"

"How come they're, twenty pounds?" asked Josh, tapping the screen and examining the charging point.

"Yeah, where are they from?" asked Aiden. "Twenty pounds is very cheap."

"Oh, contacts at the factory – you know, they sell off the seconds, the ones with damaged cases or boxes. We buy them – pass on the saving. Hello, love," the woman said to Ava.

"Hi," she said, hanging back.

"Xarca. The same make as the VR headsets," Chloe muttered.

"Have you got the money, then?" asked the woman, looking doubtfully at Josh.

Josh reached into his pocket. Aiden knew he

didn't have any. "Left it at home," he said, glancing up at Aiden and pointing at the word *Xarca*.

Aiden nodded his head, wondering if Josh had made the connection between the phones and the headsets. "That's a pity," he said, trying to catch Josh's eye.

"But I could come back for one," said Josh to the woman. "If you were here later?"

Just then Grandma arrived on the quayside. She strolled over to the woman's stall. "Twenty pounds for a mobile phone? That's very good," she said. "Can I have a look? Mine's rather ancient. Could do with something that can take a picture. What do we think, Aiden – bargain?"

"Grandma – er, can I have—?" started Aiden.

"Here you are, madam." The woman handed her one of the mobiles. "Very high quality, seldom seen in these parts. Any questions?"

"Xarca, Aiden. Xarca," said Josh. "Same company."

"Yeah, yeah, we know," said Ava, "but we're thinking—"

"About the fires," hissed Chloe.

Grandma was deep in conversation with the

woman. "Will it need charging before use? I do find that an awful nuisance."

"Do you think they're the same people?" whispered Aiden.

"I dunno," said Josh. "It was a man with a mushroom head earlier, not a frog woman."

"What?" laughed Chloe.

"Yeah – his haircut was like a mushroom – or a jellyfish. Anyway, he said he'd run out of headsets and packed up and rushed off, not before that horrible girl bought one and then, like half an hour later – this frog woman appears!"

Aiden looked over to the stall. The woman did have a froggyness about her. Perhaps it was the green jacket and trousers. Or perhaps it was the slimy way she talked.

"It was like – he went, she came. Like Superman and Clark Kent but more disappointing."

"Dur, Josh. Obviously one was a man and one was a woman," said Ava, "but is it the same actual stand? Same table, same rubbish little plastic chair?"

"Is it the same van?" Aiden steered Josh round in a circle until he could see the back of the van.

"No," said Josh, rummaging in his pocket and pulling out his red notebook. "Different number plate – see?"

Aiden looked over Josh's shoulder. "Except…" The letters of the number plate were the same, but in a different order. Josh had written *WR51 TUP*. The number plate of the van parked in front of them was *TR15 WUP*. "It's like an anagram."

"A what?" said Josh.

"You know," said Chloe, "when you mix up the letters to make a different word, like in crossword puzzles."

Josh looked completely blank.

"Do you remember anything about the van apart from the number plate?" muttered Aiden.

"White…" Josh stared into the middle distance and strained his memory. "With some yellow…"

"String hanging off the back door?" asked Chloe.

All four of the cousins walked casually over to the van. There was a yellow string flapping in the breeze.

"Ta-da!" said Ava. "But did you actually see the headsets?"

Josh shook his head. "Only boxes."

"Now what?" asked Ava.

"Now we definitely get the police. Even if the headsets aren't anything to do with the fires, there's something really odd going on," said Chloe. "I'll run down to the hotel – see if there's still a police officer there. Keep that woman here."

Aiden looked back at the woman. She was taking a twenty-pound note from Grandma and handing her a phone in a box. "No charger, I'm afraid, but it's a micro USB, cheap as chips."

"Oh – OK," said Grandma. "Seems a bit ripe not giving a charger with it. Not even a cable?"

"That was my last one," said the woman, waving a box around. "Take it or leave it."

"But hang on, you've got loads," said Josh stepping forward. "What about those?"

"Oh, they're empty boxes. Just for merchandising, see." The woman glanced along the quay towards the harbour-master's office. "Just going to pack myself away." She was suddenly in a hurry. Aiden looked round and saw Chloe at the far end of the harbour arguing with a figure in uniform.

"Goodness," said Grandma, standing back as the woman grabbed her sign and rammed it in the back of the van. "What a rush!"

"Gotta slow her down," muttered Ava. "Josh?"

"I got it!" said Josh, running round the back of the stall.

"Wait," said Aiden, but it was too late – Josh had already taken off Bella's lead and thrown a stick over the van so that Bella's shortest route was straight through the flimsy stack of mobile-phone boxes.

"Oh dear!" said Grandma as Bella charged back the same way, sending the boxes all over the quayside.

"Sorreeee!" shouted Josh. "We'll help!" And he raced into the muddle, flinging the boxes in the general, but not specific, direction of the van. Laughing, Ava joined in, and Bella, thinking the whole thing a terrific game, charged around tossing the boxes back out of the van and on to the quayside.

"Oh, Bella!" hooted Grandma, grabbing at Bella's collar and missing.

"Stop it! Stop it!" shouted the woman. "I've got to go now."

Aiden saw her glancing along the quay towards

Chloe, as if she was waiting for something. Afraid of something?

He joined his cousins in the confusion, adding to the chaos, taking as many boxes out of the van as they put in.

"For goodness' sake!" said the woman, just as Chloe began to return along the quay, having failed to get the policewoman to follow her.

"I'll shut the door," shouted Aiden.

The woman ran for the driver's seat, which is when Josh and Ava leaped into the back of the van and slammed the door as the woman drove off, scattering Grandma, Bella, Aiden and the seagulls in her desperation to get out of Drake's Bay.

CHAPTER 9

Brother and sister stared at each other across the sea of cardboard boxes, Ava could just see the top of Josh's head over the big piece of white cardboard that had acted as a sign.

"Josh," she said, "why did you do that?"

"You jumped first," he said. "I didn't want to leave you on your own."

"That's rubbish and you know it," said Ava. "I'm only here because I couldn't leave my little brother on his own in the back of a strange van."

The van lurched, and Ava shot across the back

of the space, thumping into Josh.

"Get off!" he said, rubbing his elbow.

"Sorry," she said. "Like I did it on purpose."

They sat in silence, bouncing and shaking, until Ava crept to look out of the tiny square window at the back.

"Just passing Clifftoppers," she said.

She stayed staring out of the window as the countryside sped by. What had they done? They might never get back home again. This was a grade-one disaster.

"What's this?" asked Josh behind her.

"What?" She scrambled back. Josh held out a piece of paper.

Ava examined it. "It's a bill from a printer." She held it up to the light and read. "*Two hundred stick-on labels, two hundred box labels. Proofed as below.*"

"What does that mean?" asked Josh, sliding back and forth across the van.

"I'm looking at the 'proof below' – and it says 'Xarca'."

"Let's see," said Josh, examining the paper. "That's a dead copy of the Xarca logo. So they've been sticking labels on boxes? Why would you do that?"

"Let's see." Ava picked up one of the mobile-phone boxes and slipped her fingernail under the corner of the label. She peered underneath. "Just an address – definitely not England. Nothing to do with Xarca."

"So they're not real. The phones."

Ava shook her head. "No. But they're pretending they are – whoa!" The van suddenly halted and Ava fell, sprawled across the back of the van.

"Quick, hide," said Josh, throwing cardboard cartons over his head until he more or less disappeared.

"There's nothing to hide under!"

Josh chucked over a large flattened cardboard box and she tunnelled beneath it, holding her breath and trying to keep still.

The engine stopped, and then Ava heard the click of the driver's door opening followed by the crunch of gravel. *Where are we?* she thought to herself. *A layby somewhere?*

And then voices.

"How long you been waiting?" said Frogwoman.

"Not too bad. I walked over from the bus stop.

Be glad to stop lugging this lot around though." A man's voice.

Ava felt the vibration as the door by her foot opened. She held her breath, but all that happened was that someone put something heavy on her leg. She stayed still, waiting for the door to close, but it didn't.

"I thought you'd be longer. Why'd you leave so soon?" asked the man.

"Kids – I think they twigged. One of them went off to get a policewoman. I was lucky not to get caught."

"That's all we need. I packed up sharpish this morning but we might need to move on soon. After we've secured the next delivery."

"Delivery?" mouthed Josh.

"When's the next lot due in?"

"Another hundred and fifty this afternoon," said the man. "We're going to have to get rid of them quick."

"Where are they coming to?"

"More," whispered Josh. "There are going to be more?"

"Shh, idiot," said Ava, frantically listening, but

she'd missed it. Then the door slammed, and the feet crunched round the side of the van, and although the voices rumbled, Ava couldn't hear what they said.

"Are we off again?" whispered Josh, sitting up and spraying cardboard boxes all over the van.

"Shh," said Ava.

There was the sound of gears crunching, then the gravel and the van lurched off.

"Josh! You talked right over the most important bit," hissed Ava.

"Sorreeeee," he said. "But that was almost one hundred per cent definitely Mushroom-head – the man who was selling the VR headsets in the market."

"You sure?" Ava looked down at the box on her legs. Josh looked too. "Wonder what's in here."

"Bet it's the headsets. But it's got tape on it," he said. "You can't open it."

"So we're going to have to take it off carefully," she said, peeling up a corner and pulling the long strip from the top.

She'd just managed to remove the main piece of tape and open one flap when the van slowed, halted, and the driver's door slammed.

Feet crunched on the gravel and the handle of the back door went down.

"Right," said a voice outside. "Let's label this lot."

CHAPTER 10

Chloe and Aiden agreed to lie. Telling their grandparents that Ava and Josh were in the back of a small white van speeding across the countryside seemed like a bad idea.

"They ran after Bella," said Chloe.

"But she's right here," said Grandma, pointing at Bella who, worn out after all the excitement, had gone to sleep in the middle of the high street.

"Yeah, but she wasn't just now. Er…" Chloe looked at Aiden.

"They rushed to search for that cat between the

boat sheds," said Aiden. "I think. I didn't really see where they went."

Grandma had given them a hard stare and gone off to buy some carrots.

"How do we find out if the people in the post office had one of those headsets?" said Aiden. "Should we go down to the hotel to look for them?"

"What? While the others are missing?" said Chloe. "I think we need to tell someone – I mean, they might have gone miles." She felt more and more uncomfortable about lying.

"You're right, but it might be safer to tell Grandpa," said Aiden. "Grandma'll go ballistic."

"Hmm," said Chloe. "He's back at the farm – it'll take ten minutes to get there."

"OK. And we might find the post-office people on the way."

They started walking back to Clifftoppers. As they neared the church, Bella's nose twitched. She let out a low growl and leaped sideways. Neither of them was fast enough to grab her as she shot through the lychgate and into the churchyard.

"Hey!" shouted Aiden, but Bella wasn't listening. Her ears were flat against her head as she sped across the grass and shoved at the heavy church door.

"Bella!" Chloe raced through the lychgate and made it to the door just as Bella disappeared through it.

"It's Mr Tibbs!" said Aiden, pushing the door open and entering the cool of the church. Chloe looked round and saw the black cat balanced on the back of the pulpit, his back arched, hissing at Bella, who was unashamedly barking.

"Shh, Bella," said Chloe.

But Bella wasn't listening. The cat wasn't listening either. His eyes were focused on the dog, and the two of them looked ready to scrap.

"I'll take the dog," said Aiden, "if you can get the cat."

"Oh. Thanks," said Chloe, looking at the outstretched claws, the tiny pointy teeth and the cat's wide-eyed stare. "Thanks a lot." She leaned towards the cat, who turned towards her and gave her the same hiss that she'd given the dog.

"Shh, Bella." Aiden tried pulling the dog away from the side of the wooden pulpit. Bella let out a noise somewhere between a snarl and a sneeze and made a lunge towards Mr Tibbs. "It's just a cat," said Aiden, grasping her collar and dragging her across the floor. "You've seen plenty of cats before."

He pulled, Bella growled, and the cat hissed.

"Can you get hold of it?" asked Aiden.

The cat reminded Chloe of the sea urchins she'd seen on a holiday to Greece. Spiky, dangerous and impossible to pick up. "I'll try," she said, swallowing. She pulled the sleeves of her sweatshirt down so that they covered her hands. "Here puss-cat, come here. It's OK, that bad nasty dog isn't going to do you any harm."

The cat didn't seem to understand and opened its mouth to let out a silent hiss.

"Come on, it's fine," she said, more to herself than the cat. She climbed the wooden steps to the pulpit and reached out towards Mr Tibbs, but the cat wasn't interested. He turned his green eyes on her, leaped past her arms and landed on top of a carved angel that projected from the wall. He took a brief look at Chloe's outstretched hand and jumped into an alcove above the angel's head, hissing one last time before disappearing.

"Now what?" she said. "I can't reach. And even

if I could, I don't want to stick my hand in a dark hole with a strange cat with teeth in it. And I'm not very good at cats."

"OK," said Aiden, biting his lip. "I'll try."

It took them a moment to swap. Chloe tucked her fingers round Bella's collar and hauled her back towards the doorway. "Come on, you stupid creature." Bella was heavy and hard work, but at least she didn't have small pointy teeth or sharp claws, and she'd never bite.

From the top of the pulpit steps, Aiden looked back down at Chloe. "I don't know if I'm going to be any better than you. I can't really see him. All I can see is a dark bit, which might be him."

"Try reaching your hand in?" said Chloe. "Maybe you can hook him under his stomach."

She held her breath as he put his hand into the dark slot that Mr Tibbs was currently inhabiting at the back of the alcove. She felt a little mean making Aiden tangle with Mr Tibbs, but he was older, and taller.

"Hey, well done. I knew you'd be better than me," said Chloe. "He didn't go for you! Now see if you can get him."

Aiden reached further in. For a second his arm stayed put and then he jerked it back. "Ow! Stupid cat, I'm trying to help." He looked at his hand. Two white stripes showed where Mr Tibbs's claws had struck.

"You might have to put something over your arms?" suggested Chloe, and then immediately wished she hadn't as Aiden glared at her, rubbing his wrist. "Sorry," she said, struggling with Bella, who had suddenly developed an interest in a plastic lunch box that might or might not contain biscuits. "I was just trying to help."

Aiden pulled his jacket off and put it on back to front, so that it covered his chest and the sleeves covered his hands. Then he put his left arm up to the hole, and gently pushed into the dark.

Mr Tibbs chose that moment to leap, passing Aiden and heading straight for Chloe, who let go of Bella to catch him. Bella yelped and vanished under a pew as the wooden side of the pulpit swung open and a dark, spidery, human-sized void appeared.

"Whoa!" Chloe gripped Mr Tibbs, holding the cat under its armpits so that the flailing claws and needle teeth couldn't reach her. "What is that?"

Aiden ran down the pulpit steps and for a second all four of them were frozen, gazing into the black entrance of something that went off down a dusty staircase into the darkness.

"What shall we do with the cat?" said Aiden at the same time as Chloe said, "Have you got any battery on your phone?"

At the back of the church in the children's section they found a hamper full of dressing-up clothes. With Aiden holding Bella back with his leg and Chloe thrusting her arms deep into the princess costumes, they managed to stow Mr Tibbs and shut the lid. He let out some plaintive mews but then he went quiet and Chloe heard that funny stamping that cats do, followed by purring.

"Think he's OK," she said, and joined Aiden by the pulpit as he gazed into the black hole.

"Have you—?"

"Shh!" He held up his finger. "Listen. What can you hear?"

Chloe listened. "Voices?" she said. "I can hear voices. And seagulls?" she asked. "Is that really what we can hear?"

"And the sea?" asked Aiden, a smile creeping across his face. "Waves."

As Chloe watched, the cobwebs drifted in and out, and she realised that the hole didn't smell of damp cupboards. It smelled of the beach and the sea and seaweed.

"Ready?" asked Aiden.

Gripping Bella by the collar, Chloe took a deep breath and said, "I'm ready!"

CHAPTER 11

When the door of the van opened, Josh seized his chance and leaped. Imagining that everything behind him was out to get him, he ran through what turned out to be the forecourt of a petrol station, past Mushroom-head and Frogwoman, straight past an elderly man fiddling with his windscreen wipers, past the kiosk where a woman sat doing the crossword and on to the moor behind.

"Wait! Josh!" he heard Ava behind him, but he wasn't going to wait, and he ploughed on, dodging rabbit holes and ducking between gorse bushes until the fear that was sitting on the back of his neck subsided and he felt able to stop and breathe.

"Hey!" shouted a voice in the distance. *Mushroom-head?*

"After them!" came another voice. *Frogwoman?*

He heard car doors slam, but no engine start, and he paused to listen. Ava came crashing in behind him, breathing heavily. "We've gotta get out of here," she said. "They're following."

And they were. Behind them the bushes were moving — or, rather, someone was moving in the bushes.

"We could stay here," whispered Josh, looking around at the scrub. It was thick. Probably almost thick enough.

"Too close," said Ava, beginning to weave through the gorse at a steady trot.

"Wait for me," said Josh, but his sister obviously had no intention of waiting. So, calling her names under his breath, Josh jogged behind, heading steadily uphill to a tall pile of rocks balanced on another pile of rocks. Ava increased her speed and he lost sight of her. He'd catch her in a minute.

The landscape looked unfamiliar and as Josh ran, trying to get as far as possible from their pursuers, he had a growing sense of getting lost. He turned as he ran and realised he couldn't actually even see the petrol station any more. He couldn't see the road. He couldn't see the sun. He couldn't even see his sister.

"Ava!" he called, taking a moment to lean over and suck some air into his lungs. "Ava?"

There was no answer, so he jogged on towards the piles of stones, and then looked back. In the distance he could see cars going along a road. It might have been the road they'd been on. But then again, it might not.

"Ava!" he shouted. "Where are you?"

Still no answer.

"Ava! You utter toilet! You complete drainpipe! Where are you?"

Nothing. He scoured the moorland. Bushes, grass, bushes. Sheep. Sheep and mist. Josh didn't like mist. Ghosts hung around in mist. Didn't they?

"Ava! You're a rotten fish. A squished banana – I'll never lend you anything ever again."

His voice bounced back from the stones. But

there was no sign of Ava.

He'd been so sure she was ahead of him.

"AVA! You can't borrow any of my stuff again. Ever. And I won't give you my pizza crusts. You're a toad, a frog, a tadpole, a … a slimy thing that lives at the bottom of a pond." He paused for breath. "Where are you?!"

"Here!" said a voice behind him, and a hand fell on his shoulder.

"Aaargh!" he screamed and jumped. "I thought you were a − a…" He didn't dare say ghost.

"Not much good at running away quietly are you?" she said. "And, for your information, I am not a toilet."

Josh nearly said, "It's good to see you," but stopped himself just in time. One thing he would never admit to Ava was being worried about her, another was being scared.

"So where are we?" he asked. "And how are we going to get home?"

The mist turned to rain. Fine wet rain that closed in across the moor and made it difficult to see very far. Despite the rain, Ava was sure she knew which way to go, but she knew Josh wouldn't believe her. He really was the most annoying person in the world.

"That," she said, pointing across the moor, "is south. South must be where we came from. Drake's Bay is south."

Josh peered into the rain. "How d'you know that's south?"

"Because it is," she replied.

"With what? Your super-accurate internal compass? The one that got us lost at the shopping centre last Christmas and couldn't find its way to the car park?" said Josh. "Cos if we're using that particular piece of equipment, it's pretty rubbish."

Ava felt her face go hot at the memory. "For your information, that was because we were on the wrong floor."

"And we were on the wrong floor because?"

"Oh, shut up, Josh." Ava turned away from him and scanned the landscape. He was right, she had no real idea where south was. She just felt that it was south. It looked as if it was the right direction. If only the sun would come out, it would all be so much easier.

But the sun stayed firmly behind the clouds and

the rain came down and her sweatshirt got soaked in seconds, and then she was quite cold.

She took a deep breath. "What's your idea, then?"

"The petrol station and the road are up there," said Josh, pointing in the opposite direction. "So we should go that way."

"OK," she said. "And the people we just ran from? What if they're still there? What if they're waiting for us there?"

Josh sighed. "But it's just miles of nothing your way. Look!"

Ava looked where he was looking. It *was* miles of nothing. She felt all her energy flood out and she sat down, her back to the stones, wishing they'd brought something with them. Food, money, a map, a compass. She looked at her phone, at the GPS. There was a helpful dot in the middle of a blank screen.

"There's nothing here," said Josh.

As she stared over the lumps and bumps and bushes, the wind blew the rain to the side and through the gap in the curtain she saw something moving.

"Over there." She pointed. "Is that a car?"

Josh looked where she was pointing, screwing up his face and peering exaggeratedly into the distance. She knew he could see it. She knew he was trying to decide whether it was worth pretending that he couldn't in order to string this out. She watched the battle on his face. In the end, sense won.

"Yes. A red car. Then a blue one."

"A road?" said Ava, wishing she could windscreen-wipe the sky and see a little clearer. "Oh yes – and look! A bus!"

"I'll beat you there!" shouted Josh and he leaped from the pile of rocks, missed his footing, and fell head first into some sheep poo.

CHAPTER 12

The steps turned out to be a spiral staircase, one that hadn't been used for a very long time. In the light of Aiden's phone torch the cobwebs appeared as a white wall in front of them, so it wasn't until they'd walked quite a few paces that he realised it was a spiral staircase. It was so narrow that his elbows touched the sides, and so low that his head brushed the roof. It was also cold, super cold, down here under the church. None of this was nice and he imagined the millions of spiders that he must be picking up on the way.

"Urgh!" said Chloe.

Ahead and below he could definitely hear the sea, and the wall of cobwebs seemed to breathe — which made it even more unpleasant.

Behind him Chloe's feet tapped on the stone steps and Bella's claws made a scuffling sound. She sniffed and sneezed at the dust, but she wasn't growling or whining, which made Aiden feel bolder.

"What can you see?" asked Chloe.

"Nothing, just—"

"Don't say it," she said. "Not if you're going to say spiders."

"I wasn't. It's just all white."

"That's almost worse."

They carried on for another few seconds in silence. "I've been counting," she said. "Fifteen steps."

Aiden didn't answer. He'd been counting too — and he'd been thinking about the small table that they'd put into the gap, and hoping that it would stop it blowing shut again if someone came into the church. He'd also been thinking about the cat and the hole and just how on earth he or Mr Tibbs had managed to open the door.

"There must have been a lever," he said.

"Did you pull or push anything?"

"No," he said, puzzling and counting, until at fifty steps he lost count and the cobwebs seemed to grow greyer and the ground beneath his feet yellower. The whiff of the sea became stronger, mixed with a damp smell of sea caves and dead fishy things.

"I think we're nearly at the bottom," he said, feeling the floor of the passage change from paving to something grittier. On either side the stone walls continued, but now there were no more steps, and there was definitely some light at the other end.

"We don't need the torch any more," he said, taking off his glasses and cleaning away the cobwebs. Ahead and slightly below him was a long horizontal slit of yellow, and the cobwebs had changed from thick and white and strong, to traily and grubby, as if perhaps the spiders down here had moved on.

"Yay!" said Chloe. "I can properly see the end. Come on." She and Bella squeezed past him and charged towards the light. Aiden stumbled along the last few metres of the passage, and had to take his glasses off again to remove the last of the cobwebs. Ahead of him, Bella raced through the slot and ran back, barking. She repeated the exercise several times and then sat panting, and possibly grinning. Kneeling down, Chloe stuck her head through the hole. "We're at Fire Bay, right down low – I don't know how we never saw it!"

Aiden crouched next to her. She was right. There were some bushes in front of the entrance, and rocks, and actually, when Chloe said "low" she meant some metres above the actual beach, so it would be a scramble to get down, but for a moment they stayed there looking over to Jake and the bonfire builders and the boats coming and going from the harbour, and Pearl's kayaks lined up waiting to go out.

"We could…" started Aiden.

"Cat," said Chloe. "We can't leave it there. I'll go in front this time."

It took only a few minutes to make the return journey, and somehow the spiders' webs were less horrible this time. They reached the top of the steps and Aiden stood next to the pulpit holding the door open. "That's much quicker than walking through the village," he said, as Chloe crouched on the inside of the door, looking for a catch.

"There must have been a way of closing it from the inside. But yes, it is." She fumbled inside the spidery space, feeling for anything that might trigger the door.

"I can only think of one reason for it," said Aiden.

"Smugglers," said Chloe, peering into another spidery hole behind the door. "Do you think this is it?" She had found an old metal hook inside the hole on the wall. Somehow it looked as if it wanted to be pulled.

"Try it!" said Aiden.

"Will you get me out if it shuts? I don't want to go back down there on my own in the dark."

"Here, take my phone just in case, and I'll jam my foot in the door."

Chloe pulled the hook. It grated on the stone, but when she tried a little harder it came towards her and the door began to swing shut.

"Hey!" The door closed quickly against Aiden's foot. "Get out of there!"

"No!" Panicking, Chloe pushed the hook the

other way, and to her relief, the door reversed direction. "Phew," she said, tumbling out on to the flagstones. The door closed behind her, echoing in the church as it snapped shut.

"You're covered in cobwebs!" said Aiden.

"So are you!" And he was — swathes of grey dust-filled silk coated his back and arms, and Chloe shuddered.

"Ugh!" she said, twisting round to sweep them off. "Ugh!"

"Let's take Mr Tibbs back to his owners. If we go outside, the wind might blow some of this off."

Mr Tibbs was quite chilled when Chloe lifted him out of the basket. He stretched and settled comfortably in her arms. Bella, perhaps exhausted by her visit to the tunnel, perhaps finally bored of the cat, paid him no attention, which is how they managed to walk down the high street, shedding their ghostly trails along the way. From time to time Chloe shuddered as something tickled her neck or touched her cheek, but she clung firmly to the cat.

They passed the burned-out post office and had nearly reached the hotel where they knew Mr

Tibbs's owners were, when a bus pulled to a stop in front of them.

Josh climbed down on to the pavement. He was covered in something browny green, and was holding his arms out like he didn't want to touch anything.

"Josh!" shouted Aiden. Josh didn't turn but walked over to a low wall where he started brushing something off his arms. Chloe looked back at the bus. "Where's Ava?" she said.

She watched as a string of villagers poured from the doorway and then at the very end – Ava. "Thank you!" she said to one of the women with shopping bags. "I'll drop the money in tonight. We're so grateful!"

"No bother, dear. Found myself without the bus fare lots of times at your age – anyway, I know your granny."

"Oh! Um, if you wouldn't mind … not telling her?" said Ava, screwing up her face. "It's just … she doesn't know we went for such a long walk. She might not be very happy."

The woman winked. "Your secret's safe wi' me," she said, smiling. "Bye, Josh. Bye, Ava."

The cousins stopped and stared at each other.

"You'll never guess what we discovered!" said Josh and Chloe simultaneously.

CHAPTER 13

They met Mr Tibbs's family outside the hotel.
They'd just come back from a search of the net
sheds. Little Tom cried and grabbed the cat for a
hug and Mr Tibbs looked as if he'd quite like to
leave and go back to sitting in the hamper in the
church.

"That's so kind," said the mum.

"Wonderful," said the dad.

"Marvellous," said the mum.

"Are you all right?" said Tom, pointing at Josh.
"You've got something brown all over you."

"He's fine," said Ava.

"Ooh," said the girl. "Is that poo?"

"Bye now," said Aiden, thinking that Josh really needed rescuing, and a second later the four cousins were heading towards the beach, laughing while Josh stamped disgustedly on the tarmac in an attempt to dislodge some of the sticky gunk from his trainers.

"You'll be able to scrape it off on the pebbles! Anyway, look – we haven't told you. We found the smugglers' tunnel," said Chloe.

"What?"

"Actually, Mr Tibbs found it," said Aiden. "We were trying to rescue him from Bella."

"I don't get it," said Ava.

"Doesn't matter," said Chloe. "But the tunnel goes to Fire Bay, just like Pearl said."

"Wow," said Josh and Ava at the same time.

"Was there anything in it?" asked Josh. "Doubloons? Brandy?"

"Spiders," said Chloe. "Millions of them."

"Big as a plate, some of them," grinned Aiden, splaying his hands to show just how big they were.

"Seriously?" said Ava. "Show us!"

"It's this way," said Chloe, pointing, and they crunched on to the beach, Josh kicking up pebbles as he tried to clean his shoes. "What happened to you? We didn't tell Grandma, by the way."

"We lied for you," said Aiden, feeling quite proud.

"We," said Ava, "ended up going quite a long way across the moor, to a petrol station."

"And then got lost. Because of her…" Josh tilted his head towards Ava.

"And then caught a bus because of me," snapped Ava. "And he fell in sheep poo."

"Yeah, so – anyway, it turns out that they are together," said Josh. "Frogwoman and Mushroom-head. They're the same set-up."

"And the back of their van—"

"The white one with the yellow string," interrupted Josh.

"Is full of cardboard boxes, with some other random address on them. That's the real manufacturer. Some place that's nothing to do with Xarca."

"What?" said Chloe.

"And they've got a load of printed labels that

say Xarca – which look exactly like the real Xarca ones – that they're sticking on the boxes that aren't Xarca," said Josh. "If you see what I mean."

"So they're passing off something that isn't Xarca as Xarca?" asked Aiden.

"That's fraud," said Chloe. "Isn't it?"

"Glad I didn't buy one," said Josh.

"Glad Grandma didn't buy you one," said Chloe.

"But they've sold loads of them," said Josh. "There were masses of boxes in there, and he said something about *another* hundred and fifty – so if they did cause the fires, then there are a hundred and fifty of them out there in people's houses."

"Or a hundred and forty-eight," said Chloe, catching on, "because two have already caught fire."

"And there are another hundred and forty-eight out there that haven't..." said Aiden.

"Yet," said Josh.

"Oh yeah – and there's another 'shipment' this afternoon," added Ava.

"Where?" asked Chloe.

"We didn't hear that bit," said Ava, glancing at Josh.

"Josh!" said Chloe turning. "What about the girl on the beach, the one who told us about them in the first place?"

"Jasmine?" asked Josh.

"Did she get one? Did you see her this morning?"

They all stared at Josh. He stared at the sea wall and Aiden watched as his expressions went from hopeful to furious. "Yes – she did. She looked really smug. She walked away with the last one! And she said something – something about racing back to a chalet?"

Aiden stopped. They were still a few minutes from the cliff, and although it wouldn't take very long to explore the tunnel, it would probably take an hour – and an hour was important if the shipment was coming in today... An hour was important if people's houses were going to catch fire. And where were there any chalets?

"She must live in Sunnyday Park," said Chloe, as if she was reading his mind. "I think we should run and warn her – now!"

"You're right. I know you really want to see the tunnel, Josh, Ava – but I think we need to tell the police now. I think that if they're causing the fires, the police will want to know who the people are that are selling them. And I think we need to stop anyone else's house burning down. Where did you find the policewoman this morning, Chloe?"

"What?" said Josh, looking ready to lie down and cry on the beach. "But she's not even very nice."

"Aiden's right," said Ava. "Come on Josh, let's find the police. Chloe, Aiden – I think you need to find Jasmine – and fast."

CHAPTER 14

But as they were about to leave, Ava stopped. She pointed at a filthy blue trawler belching black smoke which had avoided the harbour and was chugging in towards the beach. "That's weird. Why's it missed the harbour?"

"Doesn't have a local registration number," said Chloe. "I don't think it's from here."

Ava watched it heading towards the shore. There was no jetty at the beach so it wouldn't actually be able to land.

"They're going to run aground!" said Aiden.

The wave on the bow of the boat changed and Ava realised that they were turning, and slowing. "You're right, they are going to run aground," she said, stepping back on to the beach and jogging towards the mountain of wood. "Perhaps they don't know how close to the shore they are!" She started to wave madly at the boat, jumping and shouting as she ran.

Behind Ava, the others crunched on to the beach until they were all stumbling over the rocks and pebbles and waving and racing across the flat sandy stretches, heading for the fishing boat and the bonfire.

"Hey! It's the tar barrels," said Josh. "See?"

Ava slowed. He was right. The back of the boat was heaped with wooden casks, some big, some smaller, and two people on board seemed ready to unload them.

Bella overtook her, galloping past, aiming for the people on the shoreline. She charged into the sea and galumphed back, stopping to shake herself and spray them all with water.

"Bella!" said Ava, stepping backwards, tripping, and falling on her bum while Bella shook the sandy seawater all over her. "Eeeew! Bella." Ava wiped sand from her face and looked over at the boat. She could see quite clearly now that there was a man and a woman rolling barrels up a ramp and over the side on to Pearl's small dinghy. Then the dinghy was dragged in on a rope and the barrels were lined up on the pebbles. Most of the barrels were light enough for one person to handle, but three of them were obviously much heavier and Jake and Pearl had to help each other to move them. All three of them had crosses marked on them.

There was shouting between the boat and the shore, and the boat chugged slowly away, while Jake left the beach and Pearl stayed with the barrels.

"But this isn't how they came last time," said Josh, sliding to a halt beside Ava.

"Don't they always come on a boat?" asked Chloe.

Aiden shook his head. "No, last year Jake drove them in from somewhere."

"They're all different sizes this year, and they're going to have to get them up to the church somehow," said Ava.

"Some of them look really heavy," said Chloe.

"That man," said Josh, slowly peering towards the boat as it headed out to sea.

"What man?" asked Ava.

Josh stared harder. "Nah – nothing."

"What about the woman on the boat?" asked Aiden. "Anyone recognise her?"

"S'not Frogwoman," said Josh. "Frogwoman's got blonde hair. This one's got dark hair – unless Frogwoman has a sister – or she's a shape-shifter or..."

"Or she's wearing a wig," said Ava.

"You wouldn't wear a wig on a boat. Too windy," said Aiden. "I'm imagining things."

Ava stared at the people on the boat until they became tiny dots. Something was bothering her too, but she couldn't make it add up. She was bothered by Pearl and Jake, the strange boat, the barrels – kind of excited and terrified about carrying one tomorrow, and wondering if Grandma would let her. But she was also tired. They had walked miles, and she was hungry, and now she was wet and covered in sand. She sighed. It was time to warn Jasmine, find the police, and then they could eat something delicious and explore the tunnel.

"Give us a hand up," she said to Josh, who pulled slightly harder than was necessary and left Ava staggering forward over the shingle. "Josh!"

"You asked," he said, doing his innocent smile. The one that made Ava want to put salt in his cereal.

"Hey, look," said Chloe, pointing towards the harbour. Jake's pickup bobbled slowly towards them, trying to avoid a policeman wandering down on to the beach. The policeman headed past the cousins straight towards Pearl and the barrels.

Ava watched as Pearl looked up at him and then stopped, hands on hips, while he struggled over to her.

Ava brushed the sand from her legs and wandered over so that she could join the conversation. Aiden came with her and they stood nearby, listening.

"What you after then?" Pearl asked the policeman.

Ava nearly interrupted but decided the policeman might take her more seriously if she didn't.

"'S'cuse me madam." He'd arrived out of breath

and spoke to Pearl in little huffs. "We're just making some enquiries. Have you or any of your lovely children here purchased a —" he consulted his notebook — "virtual-reality headset from a market stall in the last few days? Xarca was the brand."

"They're not mine!" laughed Pearl. "And I wouldn't know what virtual reality was if it jumped up and hit me in the face!"

Ava opened her mouth to speak. "Why?" interrupted Josh. "I wanted to, but the man sold out. I tried this morning."

"Ah — and did you see him? Would you be able to describe him?" The policeman turned to Josh.

"Yes, I would," said Josh, pulling his little red notebook out of this pocket. *"Hairy, mushroom-head hair, rude, grey eyes, yellow teeth."*

The policeman looked at his notebook. "Mushroom? Interesting. Someone else said he looked like he had a bowl cut — is that what you mean?"

Josh nodded vigorously.

"And did you by any chance see the van?"

Ava and Josh looked at each other.

"Yes…"

"And?" The policeman looked expectant.

"We…" said Josh.

"Got very close," said Ava. "Very close indeed."

"And we took their number plate."

"But they changed it," said Ava.

"They?" asked the policeman, taking off his cap and rubbing the top of his head. "There was more than one?"

"Frogwoman," said Chloe.

"Frogwoman?" asked the policeman, scribbling frantically. "Who is Frogwoman? Can you describe her?"

"She looked like a frog and was selling phones," said Josh.

"And Grandma bought one," said Chloe.

"And where does Grandma live?" asked the policeman gazing at the muddle in his notebook.

"Up at Clifftopper Farm," said Chloe.

Pearl pointed up the hill. The policeman nodded. "I know it," he said.

"But why?" asked Aiden. "Why do you want to know?"

"Because of the fires," said the policeman. "We believe, or rather the fire officer believes, that they're connected."

"Did the people at the post office buy one?" asked Chloe.

"They did – and it was upstairs when the fire started."

"I knew it!" said Josh.

"*You* knew it?" chorused Aiden, Ava and Chloe.

"You were the one who was going to buy one!" said Ava.

"Well, I'm glad I didn't. Now we know that they're—" Ava glared at her brother. And a small silence grew larger.

The policeman stared at them. "I've got a feeling that you lot know a whole bunch more than you're telling me."

CHAPTER 15

Josh was all for heading back to the farm through the secret tunnel, but the others persuaded the policeman that he needed to visit Jasmine's house before meeting Grandma. It didn't take terribly long to walk up to the caravan park but Josh was starving, tired, and covered in sheep poo.

"Well, now what?" he asked, waving his arm at the neat line of chalets that stretched all the way up the gentle slope. "How do we know which one she lives in?"

"Knock on doors," said the policeman, heading

off to the first one in the line. "Start off at the other end, kids – someone'll know her."

Letting out a long and extra noisy sigh, Josh followed Chloe up the steps of one of the chalets. It was wooden and neat and had little wellington boots planted with flowers all round the shiny red front door, which nobody answered.

"Next one," said Chloe, all chirpy and VERY annoying.

The next one was obviously not occupied. It was boarded up with grubby windows. Josh didn't even bother to climb the steps.

"Come on, Josh," said Chloe. "This is important!"

With a groan Josh marched up the next set of steps and banged on the door. Inside, he heard someone shout, and then footsteps ran to the door and it was opened by Jasmine. Seeing Josh, she immediately frowned.

Josh frowned back.

Jasmine frowned harder.

"We've found her!" Chloe shouted to the others.

Josh screwed up his face into the frowniest frown he could muster.

"Hello!" said Jasmine's mum over her daughter's

head. "You're the boy from the beach!"

"I am," said Josh, and shot Jasmine's mum his most dazzling smile. "And you're the people who bought the last VR set."

"Oh, was it the last?" said Jasmine's mum. "I didn't know — but we can't make it work anyway. I tried ringing to complain, but I can't get through on the number on the box"

"It doesn't work?" said Josh, suddenly feeling a whole lot less cross. "Brilliant!"

Jasmine scowled.

Josh punched the air, danced a little jig and stuck his tongue out at the world in general. "Justice" was the word that ran through his head. Natural justice.

After the policeman had spoken with Jasmine and her mum and taken the VR away, and they had all trudged back to the farm, the policeman sat down with Grandma. She took out the box and the phone and laid them down on the kitchen table. "See?" said Grandma. "All very shiny and new."

The policeman examined everything, and then

looked at the box, peeling up the corner of the Xarca label and examining underneath. "I'm very sorry to tell you, but I think this is a fake."

"Oh no! I've been had! Oh, Edward – I'm an idiot."

Grandpa Edward beamed and began to pour sugar into a saucepan. "Don't worry, Primrose. Could happen to anyone."

"I'm afraid, madam, you have been had," said the policeman, pulling out his notebook. "Could you describe the woman you bought it from?" he asked.

Josh pulled the sugar bowl over and stirred shapes into the white grains.

"She was wearing green and had ... blonde hair – oh, Josh, you talked to her."

"Yeah, Frogwoman," said Josh, wishing that he didn't have to keep on saying it. Surely the policeman had got the message by now. The woman was froggy.

"Did she look anything like this?" asked the policeman, tapping his phone and holding up a picture of three people.

All the cousins peered at the tiny photo. "That's

her!" shouted Josh. "And that's Mushroom-head."

"Yeah, I agree," said Ava. "That's her, but the rest of us never saw him – not even—" Josh kicked her under the table. There was no way he wanted Grandma to find out about them sneaking off in the van. She would send them home, and then he'd never get to go down the secret tunnel.

Ava glared at him and he glared back. "We overheard them," said Ava.

"How d'you mean?" asked the policeman.

"Um." Ava looked around frantically.

"At the market," said Chloe. "We overheard them at the market – on their phones. Talking about another shipment coming in today. Another hundred and fifty, wasn't it?"

"Where?" asked the policeman.

"Dunno," replied Ava. "Josh talked over that bit."

"How did you overhear them if you never saw them?" asked Grandma, staring hard at Ava.

Which was when Josh tipped the sugar bowl across the table, leaned over to correct it and upset a vase of flowers, which shot icy water all over his sister.

"Sorry," he said, dabbing at the table with a tea towel and making it worse. "So sorry."

Once she'd got over the shock, Ava smiled at him. So did Chloe. Aiden didn't even seem to have noticed. "Can I see that?" he asked, taking off his glasses and looking closely at the picture. "I've seen this man too," he said, pointing at the third man in the photo. "I just don't know where."

Grandpa had made toffee apples. "To walk to the bonfire with," he said. The toffee apples sat on a piece of greaseproof paper. The sugar pooled across it like glass. Josh snapped one off first and the rest of them followed. Even Grandma had one. They were delicious – sharp apple bitten through the crunchy golden layer of toffee, which cracked perfectly. The best Chloe had ever had, and everything would have been just fine if she could stop feeling guilty that they hadn't told the policeman everything. Because Ava and Josh had sneaked off in the van it didn't feel right to say anything about the way they'd overheard the conversation about the shipment. Still, perhaps it didn't matter. They had no idea when or where it was due in. It might be nowhere near Drake's Bay. It might not happen.

"Have you asked Grandma about carrying the barrel yet?" Chloe asked Ava.

Ava shook her head. Chloe saw her look anxiously at Grandma, who was putting on a second pair of socks and trying to stop Bella from eating her toffee apple.

"Not sure I'm flavour of the month – she knows we didn't overhear them at the market. She knows we're lying," she whispered. "She might say no."

"I'm sure she'll say yes," Chloe said.

"Now would be a good time to ask," said Aiden.

"What do you want to ask me?" said Grandma, chipping sugar from the countertop.

"Um, Grandma," said Ava, her voice rather higher than usual, thought Chloe. "How d'you feel about me carrying a barrel this evening?"

Chloe looked across at Grandpa. He was nodding as if it would be perfectly fine.

Grandma looked up from her socks. "Ah, Pearl asked you – she asked me too. Thing is, do you *want* to? You don't feel you have to, you know, to prove something? To look brave – we all know you're brave."

Ava wrinkled up her nose. "Prove something? No – I just want to run through the village with a flaming barrel on my head – I mean, who wouldn't?"

"OK then." Grandma picked at Ava's braids. "Make sure you wear a hoodie, with the hood up, OK? I'd hate to end up sending you back to your parents with no hair on your head."

"You mean I can?"

"Of course. If your grandfather agrees, I think you're perfectly capable of doing the barrel run."

"Yay!" said Ava, doing a little jump and running upstairs to find something to tie her hair with.

"It's completely unfair," said Josh.

Everyone ignored him.

"And put on your old jeans and trainers," yelled Grandma up the stairs. "You don't want to ruin your clothes!"

Ava reappeared in record time, wearing a grubby green sweatshirt of Grandpa's.

"Ready?" asked Aiden, putting Bella on her lead, and all of them set off in the twilight, out of the farm and down the lane to the village. Ava walked alongside Chloe, an extra bounce in her step. Grandma and Grandpa walked at the front. People joined them as they neared the village, flowing out of the houses, until it became a procession with some carrying flaming torches and others snapping glow sticks.

Overhead, a sliver of moon hung in the sky and distant lights glittered further out at sea. People in the crowd murmured, their voices subdued, but somehow the air tingled with anticipation. To Chloe, there was something magical about it.

"Oooh, isn't it lovely?" said Ava.

"Aren't you scared?" asked Chloe.

"Little bit," whispered Ava. "But don't tell Josh."

"I am so looking forward to this!" said Josh. "Although they've made a major mistake not letting me carry a barrel! Church?"

"Hmm," said Aiden. "Yes, church." Chloe could see that in spite of the excitement, Aiden was distracted.

"What is it?" she asked.

"It's really annoying. I recognise the woman in the pictures the policeman showed us," he said.

"She was definitely the person who was selling the phones. But why do I recognise the third person who *isn't* the mushroom-head man with the VR sets? I don't get it."

"I don't know," said Chloe, thinking that Aiden was right to be bothered. "But it's the police's problem now. Let's just enjoy Ava carrying a barrel and watch the fireworks. Look!"

CHAPTER 16

They were level with the church, where a massive crowd had formed. There was lots of cheering and laughing and shouting and people brandishing their flaming torches.

A huge cluster of barrels stood just inside the church, and Jake was rolling them out, one at a time.

"Ah – here she is – been waiting for you. C'mon Ava, love," said Pearl, beckoning her from the crowd.

"Go on," Aiden said, smiling in encouragement,

and Ava stepped forwards, horribly aware of everyone staring at her.

"What do I do?" she muttered quietly to Pearl.

"S'all right, it'll be like riding a bike, you'll get it as soon as you do it."

Ava wasn't quite so sure that carrying a flaming barrel on your head was at all like riding a bike. In fact, all the confidence she'd had five minutes earlier had utterly deserted her. Everyone standing by a barrel was about a foot taller than her and looked like they knew what they were doing.

And there were flames, loads of flames. At the moment they were on sticks, but there was a load of gloopy tar and a huge ladle, and Jake was bashing the tops of the barrels in and slopping tar around the insides.

"Here," said Pearl, handing her an enormous pair of what looked like oven gloves. "They'll keep your arms and hands from burning."

"OK," said Ava, sliding the huge mittens on to her hands.

"And this hat, it'll keep your head safe."

Pearl handed her a grubby white woven hood thing. Ava put it on and the world went quiet. It covered her head and shoulders. Now she didn't know what she was doing and she couldn't hear properly.

To her left, Jake was climbing on to a barrel, and he began addressing the crowd.

"Welcome to the Drake's Bay Fire Festival. Now, everybody – this is real fire. We expect everyone to take care, and only designated barrel carriers may go near the barrels. We have a fire officer here to make sure."

A woman in a red boiler suit stepped forward. People cheered. Ava was quite pleased to see the fire officer. She wondered where the fire extinguisher was.

"You know what the carriers must do!" A great shout went up from the crowd and Bella joined in, barking. "We will light the barrels, and then, carrying them on their heads, the runners will take the barrels to light the bonfire at Fire Bay! Step forward, first three fire carriers!"

Three men in white shirts with white hat things stepped out of the gloom. Ava hung back. There was no way she wanted to be the first runner – not without watching someone else first. It wasn't like she didn't know what would happen, but she'd never paid much attention to the details.

The crowd cheered.

"So, are you ready to run?"

"Aye, we are!" they shouted.

There was more cheering and shouting and general laughter while the fire officer went round and checked their mittens, hats and jackets and tucked them into each other. She gave Jake a thumbs up. It briefly occurred to Ava that being a barrel runner was a complete fashion disaster, but it was nearly dark, and wearing all this stuff, no one would ever recognise her.

"Time for the fire!" yelled Pearl, and she lit the first barrel. For a second nothing happened, then the flames licked around the tarry inside and small sparks began to fly as the wood beneath caught.

"First?" yelled Jake, and a white-jacketed figure hoisted the barrel up to his shoulder and swung round so that sparks scattered the crowd.

Jake lit the second and the third, and helped the carriers position them on their heads. Flames licked over the strange white mittens and, crackling, the barrels mushroomed into full flame.

There was laughing and the crowd parted to leave room for the first three barrel carriers to reach the high street.

"Run!" shouted the people. "Run!"

Ava stood with her mouth open, watching as the first barrel runners vanished down the high street, spewing fire over the crowd, which melted like butter in front of them. Hooting followed them as they ran and half of the people disappeared.

"This is insane," she muttered.

"Still wanna do it?" said Pearl next to her.

"Definitely," said Ava.

"Next!" shouted Jake.

Ava stepped forward.

Jake chose a smaller barrel and knocked the top out of it. "Ready?" He looked up at her as he slopped the tar around the inside.

She nodded. For just a second she thought about saying no, but she knew she'd really regret it if she did. Checking her braids were tucked under the hood, she crouched by the barrel as Pearl lit it. The flames took hold really quickly and although it was small it still produced a lot of sparks.

"Go!" said Jake. "Run fast — it's small, it'll burn

through quicker!"

"What?" said Ava.

"Just go!" shouted Pearl.

Using the ridiculous mittens, Ava hoisted the flaming barrel on her head and, running like a turtle, turned towards the church gate. From under the hood she saw Grandma and Grandpa cheering, and then she began to run, passing Chloe and Bella first, the flames darting all around her head.

"Ow!" she shouted to no one as the heat from the barrel began to make its way through the gloves.

She sped up as she turned into the high street, running down past the post office, her shoes bouncing off the cobbles. She nearly slipped as she dodged the postbox, and had to slow down to avoid people standing in the street.

"Run! Run!" yelled the crowds alongside.

"Get out of the way then!" she shouted back.

Space opened in front of her as the street widened and the harbour came into sight. Water. Lots of water.

"Run! Ava, run!" yelled someone next to her.

"Josh you idiot!" she shouted at him, her words vanishing in the crowd.

She kicked harder, dodging the first barrel runners who had stopped to do something that produced clouds of sparks in front of the hotel. Her hands were now really hot, and she wondered if she was going to manage the whole distance.

"You're in the lead!" shouted Josh.

Under her feet, the ground turned from tarmac to shingle. It was harder to run on but the bonfire was in sight. Willing herself over the pebbles, she headed for the small crowd waiting by the heap.

"Put it there!" yelled a woman, pointing at a small gap at the foot of the pile of wood.

And Ava lifted the flaming barrel from her head and threw it into the bonfire.

CHAPTER 17

As Chloe watched Ava prepare to run with the barrel, she turned to Josh and Aiden. "I think the gang are here," she said very quietly. "I'm sure I spotted the woman in the crowd, but I don't want to worry Ava before she runs."

"Have you seen Mushroom-head?" asked Josh.

Chloe shook her head. "No, but I might have seen the other man from the picture. I'm not sure. He was here a second ago, fiddling with the barrels. If it's the same person."

"Are there any police here?" asked Aiden.

They looked around. "Fire officers, but no police people," said Chloe. "But there's definitely something going on with these barrels." Chloe took Bella and wandered casually over to the barrel mountain.

"We should tell Ava," said Josh, watching Chloe count.

"Better start running then," said Aiden, as Ava charged out of the churchyard.

He began neck and neck with Josh. They raced each other, feet skimming over the tarmac, leaping on and off the pavements, everything around them a whirl of sparks and shouts and flames.

"Me!" yelled Josh, whipping past Aiden as he avoided a family with a pushchair.

"No, me!" yelled Aiden. By charging past the rest of the people and getting to the front of the crowd they managed to get really close to the second group – or at least in reach of the trail of sparks they were leaving.

"Mind out!" said Aiden, yanking Josh back. Two runners were taking it slowly, occupying the whole width of the high street, their barrels shooting flames all over the crowd.

"Can't get past," panted Josh.

"This way," shouted Aiden, and the two of them dived down one of the alleyways that led to the quayside, still racing, bouncing off walls and leaping steps through the gloom until they could run along the quayside. There they stopped, looking back up at the village as the first three waves of barrels came down, each surrounded by flaming torches that reflected the mass of watching faces.

"Wow!" said Aiden.

"There's Ava," yelled Josh, dodging round some lobster pots and heading towards the hotel where some kind of fire dance was taking place with the first three runners.

Josh shot off ahead and joined his sister just before the hotel.

Aiden caught up a second later. Ava was doing really well, but her barrel was burning through. In fact, it wasn't really barrel shaped any more.

"Fire! Fire!" chanted people around them. "On to the bonfire!" they shouted, Aiden stopped as Ava rolled her barrel on, shoving its remains into the bottom of the pile. Everyone went quiet. For a moment nothing happened. Someone murmured alongside him. "Just wait, just wait – it'll go."

It took almost a minute, but then the little flames left the barrel and crept along the lengths of driftwood surrounding it. The fire spat and crackled and soon it leaped to spread across a whole side of the heap.

"Hurrah!" shouted the crowd. Then another four barrels were bowled across the shingle. Small flames burst across the wood, and when another three barrels arrived, at least half the pile was alight.

"Yay!" shouted Josh, watching the sparks shooting high into the sky.

Someone dropped their barrel a long way before the fire and it took ages to roll all the way there, so long it had practically extinguished, but it made it before more arrived.

"There can't be many more left," said Aiden.

Josh glanced up the street. "I can see six more."

Just then Chloe and Bella arrived. By the light of the fire Josh could see the excitement on Chloe's face. "Isn't it fantastic? So many people," she said. "How was it, Ava?"

"Hot," said Ava, stepping back from the bonfire

and shaking off her hood and giant mittens.

"You were really brave," said Chloe.

"I'd have done it quicker," said Josh.

"I'm not even joking, Josh – no way. There were all these people in the way – babies and pushchairs and that. I didn't want to kill anyone!" Ava shook her hair out from the hood and some fragments of charcoal cascaded on to the pebbles.

"It looked amazing!" said Chloe. "The whole thing. But…" She paused.

"Not all the barrels have come down," said Aiden.

"So?" said Ava.

"And I saw the woman – the Xarca woman. She's definitely here," said Chloe.

"And Mushroom-head – she saw Mushroom-head," said Josh.

"They're definitely up to something, they wouldn't be here otherwise – they'd be waiting for their shipment. Oh! The shipment! Ship-ment," Chloe paused. "You don't think…?" Ava stared at Aiden. Aiden stared at Chloe. Chloe stared at the bonfire.

"Did the big ones with the crosses on come

down? I never saw them go past, I don't think," said Aiden.

"I know it was really chaotic back there, with people dancing round outside the hotel, but…" said Chloe, "I'm pretty sure they're still in the church."

"The three heavy ones – they're heavy because they're full of stuff," said Ava. "Let's tell the police."

Chloe shook her head. "They aren't here – the fire officers are, but there are no police at all, I checked with Pearl. She said they were busy searching the moor for dodgy virtual-reality headsets. There'll be one or two later on."

"Oh no!" said Ava. "But that's going to be too late."

"We need to get back up there," said Aiden. "We'll have to find a way through the people."

"It's too slow – they'll be gone by the time we reach the church." Ava pointed at the crowd, which stretched up the hill and into the narrow high street.

"We know a way, don't we, Bella?" said Chloe. "Follow me."

CHAPTER 18

Chloe led the way towards the arch at the end of the beach. They had to skirt past the crowds, but no one was watching them. The bonfire was too spectacular.

Bella seemed to know exactly where they were going and took Chloe over the rocks, dodging around the bushes and boulders in front of the entrance. There was no need for a torch – the bonfire lit the cliffs beautifully – but the inside looked awfully dark. It was cold out on the beach, but Chloe could feel a draught from the entrance to the tunnel that was even colder. A spidery, mouldy draught.

"C'mon," she said to Josh, and stepped into the entrance. Then she stopped. Even though Bella seemed quite comfortable and was straining to get further, Chloe couldn't see a thing.

"Dark," said Josh. "Er... Are you sure?"

"Aiden? Ava?" Chloe called over her shoulder.

"Torch, sis?" said Josh.

"What? In case there are any ghosts?" asked Ava.

"Shut up," said Josh, sounding, thought Chloe, genuinely nervous.

"There aren't any ghosts – there's nothing to be scared of. Honestly."

"'Cept spiders," said Aiden quietly.

A bright light came on suddenly behind her, and Chloe felt the phone pressed into her hand. She shone the torch into the tunnel. The spiders' webs garlanded their way forward, but this time with a black hole through the middle.

"Run," said Josh, practically hugging her. "Go."

Chloe went, ducking her head right down into her shoulders, her mouth clamped shut, trying not to think about the millions of spiders hanging around her head and neck. It took a minute to reach the steps, and then she began to climb.

Her legs started to ache, but she hung on to Bella's lead and kept on stepping, round and round, and higher and higher, Josh's breathing getting louder all the way. Her thighs were burning with the effort. *Not much further*, she thought, and then quite suddenly Bella stopped and Chloe saw the back of the door and felt the space of the pulpit open up above her head.

"We're here!" she shouted, shining the torch around until she found the metal hook in the wall that she knew should open the door. Reaching up, she slipped two fingers through and gave it a yank. It grated on the stone but nothing happened.

"What?" said Chloe. "Why didn't it open?"

"Try again," shouted Aiden.

"Are we trapped?" asked Josh. "Oh no, I can't walk through that spider tunnel again."

Chloe pulled on the hook. Again, nothing happened.

"Ugh, these spiders!" Ava's voice came up the

stairs and Chloe heard her feet stamping on the stone.

"Wait!" said Josh. "'S'cuse me." Chloe ducked as he brushed past and banged on the door, which creaked open. "Yay!" he shouted, bundling into the church, frantically beating and brushing at his head and his sides. "We're outta there!"

"What the—?" A man stood in the doorway of the church, one of the three huge barrels in front of him.

"Oh!" shouted Josh, and Chloe realised that this was mushroom-head man.

"You!" The man pointed at Josh. "And you!" Chloe turned. The man was pointing at Ava.

"What is it?" said a female voice, and the blonde-haired woman who had been selling the mobile phones appeared in the doorway. "It's those kids!"

Chloe backed towards the pulpit, Josh right at her side, while Bella growled.

A third person, a man Chloe had never seen before, appeared behind the other two. "Who are they?" he said.

"The man in the photo," muttered Aiden.

"Was he on the boat?" Chloe said quietly, her voice hidden by Bella's growling.

"Think so," said Aiden.

"Hello!" said Chloe brightly. "We were just going for a walk." It sounded ridiculous, but it was worth trying.

"What? Here in the dark?" asked the new man.

"No you weren't," said the woman. "Get 'em!" she shouted, and the men sprang forward.

Josh vanished down the tunnel, Ava followed. Aiden waited for Chloe and then they pulled the door shut behind them.

"Quick! Run!" shouted Aiden.

Bang.

Bang.

Bang.

It sounded as if the people above were bashing the door in. Something splintered.

"Hurry!" shouted Aiden behind her. Chloe almost fell headlong over Bella, who was just the faintest of white blobs in the almost complete darkness.

Smash. The air pressure changed, and light came down from above.

"They're through!" shouted Chloe, expecting feet on the stairs behind them at any second, but instead she heard dragging, followed by a match striking.

Oh no.

"Quick everyone – get off the ground!" she shouted, grabbing Bella and with Aiden's help stuffing her on to a ledge above her head.

"Walk up the walls," he said. "Like this!"

She copied him, using the narrowness of the tunnel, one leg on either side, creeping up until her head was pressed against the ceiling, leaving what she hoped was a big enough gap under her feet.

It took maybe a minute, but then the barrel came through. It was small, like the one that Ava had carried, but it was well and truly alight. As it tumbled down the staircase it lit the draped cobwebs on either side, little flames racing up and dying all around it, sparks bouncing up against the walls, showering Chloe's feet but luckily not burning them. She saw it race past.

"Ava! Josh!" she yelled.

There was shouting below, and then silence, just the distant sound of the bonfire.

"Shhh," said Aiden. "Wait."

Ava and Josh had no idea what was coming their way. They were nearly at the beach when Josh heard Chloe shout, turned and saw the flaming barrel bounding down the passage towards them.

"Jump!" yelled Ava.

Josh threw himself sideways and into the air, grabbing his sister and hoping to jump clear of the flames. Instead, they fell through a curtain of cobweb into a void – a huge empty cave that was hidden at the side of the tunnel.

"Argh!"

"What? Seriously, Josh – what is this?"

The barrel crashed against the entrance, and for a moment burning cobwebs lit the void. All Josh could see was dark shapes in a dark space, and although part of him was saying there's no such thing as ghosts, quite a big part of him was telling him to get as far away as possible.

"I don't know," he said quietly.

"Nor do I," said Ava. "But I think we need to get back up above the church if we're going to stop those guys getting away. They're probably still at the top of the tunnel. No one else is going to do it – it's up to us. *We're* going to have to stop them."

CHAPTER 19

Ava ran. She knew that the barrels would have to leave in a vehicle, and that there was only one way out of the village if someone was driving. They would have to go up the hill, past Clifftoppers.

With Josh behind her she ran out of the bottom of the tunnel, across the beach, and headed up a path that ran parallel with the high street. She quickly realised that she wasn't going to get to the farm in time. And even if she did, she couldn't think of a way of blocking the road. There was nothing big enough to stop someone getting past. Slowing for a second, she took a tiny alley that joined the high street below Clifftoppers and above the church. Feet thundered behind her, and she held up her hand, stopping Josh just before he ran on.

"Shh," she said. Creeping forward, she listened. A strange barrel-rolling sound was coming from down the hill.

"We're ahead of them," whispered Josh, "but we gotta block the road. How?"

She looked up the hill. A road-mending lorry was parked in a lay-by.

"I wish I knew how to drive," Ava muttered.

"I can," said Josh.

Ava ignored him. "I know how it works," she said, "but I can't drive. We need Aiden. We need to get them out of the church."

Aiden and Chloe waited for what seemed like forever.

"Can you hear anything?" whispered Aiden.

"No," replied Chloe, her fingers clamped round Bella's jaw.

"I'm going to risk it," Aiden said, tiptoeing up the staircase and picking his way over the splintered wood and across the church.

Bella let out a tiny whine.

"C'mon," he said, approaching the open church door. "There's no one here."

"Does that mean they've got away?" Chloe whispered and then scuttled across the church, jumping at every shadow.

Aiden didn't answer, he just stepped out into the night air. Bella growled but she didn't bark, and luckily there was quite a bit of noise coming from the bonfire celebrations. Someone was now playing the bagpipes. Perfect.

They crept out of the churchyard until they could see up and down the hill. The white van sat just a little further up the road, engine running. Three figures were struggling with something. Probably a big barrel.

"Too heavy – why don't we just take the stuff out?" came a hoarse voice. Frogwoman?

"Nah – this way if we get stopped you can't see it," said a man.

Chloe couldn't see him clearly enough, but it

might have been Mushroom-head. There was also the third man. Bearded and big, he was lifting a barrel into the van on his own while the other two were struggling. Bella strained at her lead and Chloe dragged her backwards. "Shh, Bella." Luckily the three people were too busy to notice her and Aiden, but they were going to be ready to go soon.

She looked up the street beyond the van. Was that Josh's silhouette she saw crossing the lane? And was that Ava, beckoning them round to the lay-by?

The window of the lorry was slightly open. Ava gave Aiden a leg up and he slithered through the gap until he was sitting in the driver's seat. But, of course, there were no keys.

He put his hands on the steering wheel. The lorry felt awfully big. It seemed far too high and he wondered if it was at all the same as his dad's car. He looked at the slight slope. It ought to be enough if he just took off the handbrake.

"Aiden?" Ava looked up at him through the window. "All you have to do is jam it across the road. There are walls on both sides, they can't get anywhere."

"I can do this," he said, sounding braver than he felt.

He clicked the little button on the end of the handbrake and nothing happened. He pulled it up again. He looked down to the right. The white van was still sitting there, lights on and engine running.

He did three deep breaths in and out, trying to calm himself, but his heart was beating like a bird's.

Of course. It was in gear. He needed to depress the clutch. Easier said than done, as although Aiden was tall, he was obviously much shorter than the lorry driver. Having thrust his leg down, he found the pedal and pressed at the same time as fighting with the enormous gearstick to his left. "The middle," he said to himself. "I need to find the middle."

"Aiden, hurry," said Ava.

"I'm going to get out of the way," said Josh, vanishing. Then Ava and Chloe vanished too.

Aiden found the middle of the gearbox, put the lorry in neutral and tried the handbrake again. This time, much to his delight and terror, the lorry rolled forwards. It headed silently and steadily towards the other side of the road, straight for a brick wall. Aiden frantically pulled the handbrake and the lorry slowed to a stop a few centimetres from the other side.

"Yes!" he shouted, jumping from the driving seat just as the engine revved on the hill below.

"They're coming!" shouted Ava.

"They can't get through," said Aiden.

The van headed up the hill towards them, gathering speed. The driver didn't spot the lorry until the last possible second.

Screeeech!

The driver jammed on the brakes and reversed.

"They're going to go back down the hill!" shouted Chloe.

"But they can't get out," replied Ava.

"We've got them!" said Josh. "Unless…"

The doors of the van burst open and three figures ran for the sides of the road, one towards the low stone wall of Clifftopper Farm, one towards the lighthouse, and one back down the hill.

"Right!" shouted Josh, already in pursuit of the one who was heading towards Clifftoppers.

Aiden followed him, leaping the low wall. "You can't get anywhere!" he shouted, but the figure didn't stop, ploughing on towards the house.

"Chickens – head them off towards the chickens!" hissed Josh.

Not having the faintest clue why, and a little slowed down by not being able to see a thing, Aiden ran towards where he hoped the chicken house was.

The figure ran straight towards the chicken house, Josh hot on their tail. And then suddenly they seemed to stop. "Ow!" A woman shrieked. "What the—?"

"Electric fence," said Josh.

She had run into the tangle of wire, which was invisible in the dark, and now she was getting the full fury of Grandpa's ancient fox-prevention system.

"Get me out of this – ow!" shouted the woman. "Ow! That really hurt!"

"Quick!" said Aiden. "Tarpaulins – from the shed – the ones with the chicken poo on them."

"On it!" yelled Josh and he raced off to return with something large and noisy and really quite smelly. It took them only a minute to throw it over the person struggling with the electric fence and bring her to the ground.

CHAPTER 20

On the other side of the road, Bella gave chase. She gave chase so effectively that the first man ran for the only tree in the large field leading to the lighthouse.

"Help! Mad dog!" he shouted, which made Bella even more excited.

"Ace!" shouted Ava, and she ran towards the tree, watching as the man struggled and failed to climb it, reaching halfway before he became hooked on a branch.

"Need some help?" said Ava, jogging to a stop.

"Get that dog off!" he shouted.

"She's not really doing anything."

"I just want to go home," said Mushroom-head, wriggling, and getting more entangled in the branch that seemed to be caught in his trouser belt. She leaned down and unclipped Bella's trailing lead.

"I think we'd really like you to stay where you are. So I'm just going to make sure," she said wrapping the lead round the man's flailing feet and gradually pulling them together. "We'll just knot them like this " she tied his feet together — "and leave Bella in charge while I find the police."

Chloe ran for the second man.

She knew she was on her own, but the awful possibility that he could escape in a boat kept her running even though she was terrified.

He was big, and he was in the middle of the high street. Not very fast on his feet, and not very steady. He reminded her of a bowling skittle — a pin or whatever they were called. Large in the middle and with a very small head.

Bowling!

She stopped, swung round and raced to the back

of the van. It was unlocked. "Yay," she said, as she clambered in and wriggled into the small space behind the first of the big barrels. It was seriously heavy, but Chloe braced her legs against the walls of the van and pushed as hard as she could.

The barrel slid slowly across the plywood floor and teetered on the edge of the drop. "Go on, you stupid thing!" she muttered, giving it one last shove. It tipped out of the van on to the cobbles and rolled very slowly.

"Go, barrel, go!" she shouted, willing it to pick up speed. It did, until it was quite steadily bouncing down the road. She wasted no time in getting the other two out and then, jumping down from the van, she gave both of them an extra push.

A minute later, there were three barrels gaining speed, bowling down the high street.

"Yay" she said, as the barrels seemed to take on the challenge, bouncing from side to side, careering, pursuing the person running ahead of them.

"Hey!" The man looked round, still running. The barrels were closing in on him.

"That's brilliant!" said Aiden, who had appeared by her side. "He can't get away now!"

A second later, the first barrel hit the man and sent him flying head over heels.

"Hurrah!" she shouted. The second barrel found its mark and pinned him against the postbox.

The last, the fastest and the heaviest, bounced all the way down to the beach, cut a way through the crowd, hit a large stone and finally, when everyone was staring at it, split open, spilling mobile phones in a great glittering heap just as the Fire Festival fireworks got underway.

The police officers who arrived moments later were delighted. The villagers were amazed. Pearl and Jake were embarrassed. "I thought they were very cheap and I wasn't going to turn away cut-price barrels, but if I'd known…" said Jake.

The three members of the gang were handcuffed and led to the police car, protesting their innocence, the woman still covered in chicken poo.

"We were just here for the barrel rolling – honest," shouted Mushroom-head, but no one believed them. Another police car arrived and took them away while all the fake phones and VR sets were removed from the barrels by willing villagers and handed to the police.

Afterwards, there was hot chocolate all round, and Bella, who had rather enjoyed guarding a man up a tree, barked at everyone who came near – especially Jake and Pearl.

CHAPTER 21

"Smugglers," said Grandpa, slipping a hash brown on to Josh's plate. "They were most definitely smugglers. Very clever bringing all that dodgy tech in by fishing boat. And using the village barrels – a very neat trick."

"Well done, Team Clifftoppers. Smart work," said Grandma. "Although I think some apologies may be due to the post office – that postbox may never be the same again."

"Yeah, but those barrels were brilliant bowling balls," said Josh.

"I'm sure they were," said Grandma.

"And," said Chloe, breaking the yolk on her egg, "they stopped the smuggler."

"The thing I want to see," said Grandpa, pulling more bacon from under the grill, "is the famous smugglers' tunnel. To think you found that too – Pearl will be jealous!"

"It's very spidery," said Chloe.

"And narrow." Aiden shivered.

"But if we hadn't taken it, we wouldn't have got to the top of the village in time, and they'd have got away with it," said Ava, slathering a piece of toast with marmalade and cramming it into her mouth. "And Bella, of course. She was brilliant."

Unaware of the praise, Bella took a corner of hash brown from Josh's plate while he wasn't looking.

"So, will you show me after breakfast?" said Grandpa, dishing out the bacon.

As they all walked to the church, talking about their adventure, Josh kept re-enacting the final moments of the barrel rolling so vividly that Ava had to tell him to shut up.

Grandpa led the way into the church. "Show me, then?"

"Oh goodness, look at the pulpit – it looks like it's been attacked!" said Grandma. She was right – the gang had damaged the secret door so much that it wasn't really secret any more.

"That's a bit sad," said Chloe.

"Jake'll fix it," said Grandma. "He can fix most things."

"So where's the lever?" asked Grandpa.

Aiden walked up the steps of the pulpit and pointed at the small hole where Mr Tibbs had hidden. "It was there," he said. "Somehow me reaching in triggered the door."

"How amazing," said Grandpa, peering into the alcove. "Let me just see." He reached in. "Perhaps this wooden button…"

There was a clunk, and right in front of Bella's nose the ruined door clicked open.

"Good lord," said Grandma. "All this time, and we never knew it was there."

"Right!" said Grandpa. "I've got my torch. Who's coming?"

"Mind your head, Edward," shouted Grandma

as Grandpa bashed it on the ceiling of the tunnel. Bella tugged on her lead as they carefully threaded their way down the steps.

"It was just down here," said Josh.

"What?" said Chloe.

"The hole that we fell into when the burning barrel came past."

"Oh, I'd forgotten about that!" said Ava. "It was on the left."

"No, it wasn't. It was on the right."

"Left – I swear," said Ava.

Even with Grandpa's torch, Aiden longed to get into the daylight. Even without the walls of cobwebs, there were millions of spiders.

"Here it is!" yelled Josh. "Look!"

Grandpa swung his torch through a curtain of cobwebs, brushing it aside and revealing a small cave. But not a small empty cave. A small cave filled with small barrels.

"Oh!" gasped Chloe. "Were the smugglers using it all the time? Is this more mobile phones?"

They clustered around the barrels, and Grandma ran her finger across the top of one. "I don't think so, Chloe, love. I think these have been here a very long time."

"Like, years?" asked Ava.

"Like hundreds of years," said Grandpa, digging his nails into a bung and pulling. He took a deep sniff. "Ah," he said, smiling. "Brandy. Very elderly brandy."

"Brandy?" said Aiden. "Like real ancient smugglers' brandy?"

"And look at the walls," said Aiden. "See the tide line?" He pointed at the white salty rim on the rock.

"Oh – so the sea comes in here," said Chloe.

"Or *came* in here," said Grandpa. "Look how dried out this seaweed is. I'm guessing that there's been rock falls over the years which blocked up the hole from the high tides. But it obviously used to come in here."

"And it made the barrels float," said Grandma.

"Which would explain the booming noise that they heard for so many years," said Grandpa.

"So the ghosts were just brandy barrels floating about in a big cave?" said Chloe.

"We found braaaaandy!" yelled Josh, racing past his grandparents and leaping out through the gap.

He ran towards the pile of ash that marked last night's celebrations.

"Yay!" shouted Chloe, taking off behind him, skipping over the rocks. "We found brandy and we've still got three more days!"

"How splendid," said Grandpa, helping Grandma down the rocks. "Isn't the beach a delight after that spidery hole. Imagine – all that contraband making its way up to the church."

"And a tunnel, there for so many years. Right under everyone's noses! We'll just go and tell someone about your discovery. That brandy'll be worth a fortune. Good money for the village. See you at home, children," said Grandma, taking Bella's lead and Grandpa's elbow and walking along the beach in the direction of the harbour.

Aiden wandered over to the fire. Someone had raked out all the metal bands from the barrels and the police had taken the three smugglers' barrels along with the contents. There was nothing left that showed what an extraordinary evening it had been.

"All gone," said Chloe.

"We've got the memory," said Ava. "Chloe –

when you chucked those barrels off the truck!"

"I know, wasn't that the best?" said Chloe. "And Josh and Aiden tricking that woman into the electric fence?"

"And going down the tunnel for the first time!" said Josh.

"And," laughed Chloe, "you two jumping in the back of that van!"

"It was all excellent," said Aiden, looking towards their grandparents. "It always is, here, with them."

"I know," said Ava, picking up a stone and skimming it into the sea. "Being here is sooooo good. This really is the best place in the world!"